Aryah has been writing books since the age of fourteen when her school librarian challenged her to write the type of story she was looking for. Nine years later, she is still writing stories whilst working in a primary school in her home city of London. When she isn't writing, reading or watching more TV than she probably should, Aryah likes to bake cakes, buy things she doesn't need and spend time with her family.

For all those amazing women who have always inspired me. So much so that this book came about.

Aryah

A Tale from All My Sisters

Dear Yasmin,

May your inner voice always be heard!

Best wishes,

Aryah

Austin Macauley Publishers™
LONDON * CAMBRIDGE * NEW YORK * SHARJAH

Copyright © Aryah Bukhari 2022

The right of Aryah Bukhari to be identified as author of this work has been asserted by the author in accordance with sections 77 and 78 of the Copyright, Designs and Patents Act 1988.

All rights reserved. No part of this publication may be reproduced, stored in a retrieval system, or transmitted in any form or by any means, electronic, mechanical, photocopying, recording, or otherwise, without the prior permission of the publishers.

Any person who commits any unauthorised act in relation to this publication may be liable to criminal prosecution and civil claims for damages.

This is a work of fiction. Names, characters, businesses, places, events, locales, and incidents are either the products of the author's imagination or used in a fictitious manner. Any resemblance to actual persons, living or dead, or actual events is purely coincidental.

A CIP catalogue record for this title is available from the British Library.

ISBN 9781398424357 (Paperback)
ISBN 9781398424364 (ePub e-book)

www.austinmacauley.com

First Published 2022
Austin Macauley Publishers Ltd®
1 Canada Square
Canary Wharf
London
E14 5AA

Disclaimer

All these stories are based on real-life experiences and anecdotes. Some facts have been exaggerated for effect or changed to ensure the individual's privacy. These stories still maintain the message they set out to achieve.

Women are a lot stronger than we give them credit for. When we speak to them, we learn this.

Foreword
London, England

I began thinking up the idea of this book a few months before my little sister was going to turn nine. She was going to have to start wearing a headscarf full time and I wanted to share with her the experience that many other girls had going through the same journey.

When I first started to put together this compilation of stories, I was moved by some of the things I'd read, seen or heard. The stories were different from what I was looking for, but they made me want to read or learn and know more about the women behind the masks. I took notes on a few of the stories that I came across in my notebook and thought I'd find a place for them in something else later but didn't want to let go of them just yet.

Trying to get back on task, I asked my mum more about my own family. I did not know my own grandmother, but I've always relished hearing stories about her. It was one particular story (featured somewhere in the anecdotes of this book) that made me change the direction of this book. I decided I didn't want my sister to be more conscious about wearing her headscarf; questioning whether she found some resemblance to one person or another. Instead, I wanted her to understand the strength and power that came with being a woman – especially in our current political climate. I think it is now more important than ever for women to come together and share their stories.

The main thing I took away from anything my grandmother did was that she was ever so resilient. She was not like our classic narrative of a wife, mother and daughter. She did not need anyone but herself to prop her up – although the additional support did not go in vain. My grandmother was a strong woman who was very adaptable and very courageous. I see a lot of these qualities in my mum and in turn (I hope) myself.

Grabbing my red notebook, I began to put together my notes like pieces of a puzzle. It was very important to me that these stories were about women but not all from one place. I was born and brought up in England, but I was always taught about my Pakistani heritage. I recognised many similarities between these two cultures growing up and as the things I watched on TV began to change, I felt my stories and my upbringing was very similar to so many other cultures. I wanted to ensure in this book, that these stories were not lost in translation because of where someone grew up. This happened a lot in my conversations growing up. A woman being suppressed in the Middle East was a lost cause because she was a prisoner of her religion but a suppressed woman in the West going through the same thing needed to be saved. I hope these stories show that it does not matter where you grow up or have lived, people who are struggling are the same. We are still facing the same problem just at different times (and time zones).

Researching more stories for my book, I realised that whether it be on the TV, in the news or on the radio, as a society, we still care more about the way a woman acts or what she is wearing than what she is actually doing. Women have a lot more worth than this in real life. Their lives are more complex and difficult than we see – though we do a lot of it dressed well. Although movies and TV shows have made an attempt to change the narrative, women are still very much price tagged and dated. This is not something that just stops on screen but also in the real world. A lot of unrealistic expectations are placed on women and young girls. A lot of this is because of what we see and continue to pass down to our younger generations. As well as men, women play a large role in continuing to fit themselves (and their younger daughters, sisters or nieces) into boxes that provide no breathing space. This is because they feel they have no other choice. However, things are changing, and more young women are feeling empowered to fight for their rights as they watch older women suffer through pains that should be felt by no one.

Even though she is already driving me crazy with her very loud opinions, I do not want my sister to think she has any form of barrier that should stop her ambitions and personal growth. I remember when I was growing up, I was a very *loud* child and quickly garnered the nickname 'chatterbox Aryah'. I hated the name. Although some found my chatting quirky, a lot of people close to me found it annoying and always said, "A girl should be seen and not heard." I paid no attention to this no matter how many times it was said to me, but I do remember worrying about it a lot. With so many people saying it repeatedly, I was conscious of whether I was saying something wrong all the time or being too opinionated. Thankfully, my mama allowed me to express myself freely – although it did also drive her crazy at times and I did say a lot of things I shouldn't have. I think that's why I've always found it so easy to communicate with people and express my thoughts in words. I was given the same voice as my brothers (although I used mine significantly more) and I was allowed to use it to express my opinions, my excitement, and my feelings.

I want the same for my sister. I do not want her to be narrated as the girl who asked, 'what do we do now?' in a crisis. Mainly because I have never known *any* woman to not know what to do when life begins to go sideways – no matter how much someone tries to convince me otherwise. Even now, my siblings and I (most of us sixteen and up) will ask my mum to 'do her shit' whenever we're stuck and by some motherly magic, everything seems to work or be found.

This book has tied together the stories of women all over the world and I hope that everyone finds something relatable and something to take away from each story. Although I have tried to portray a lighter side to all these stories – one full of hope and prosperity for these women, the sad truth is that this does not exist for everyone. These stories may be compiled by only one person trying to share the experiences that women go through in their lives but are by no means isolated incidences. I think we often find ourselves turning away from darker stories because they don't fit the narrative we have of our societies. It is also very easy to brush the initial problem under the carpet – especially when it's for the sake of family honour or pride. However, for women who face these issues, time is slipping away like honey in an hourglass. Although some of these stories may be altered, the body of them is very true. I wanted to shed a light on problems that people refuse to accept – and therefore don't acknowledge. Every society and culture has its own trove of stories it hides from the world as if it were a military secret. I wanted to provide a small but (hopefully) significant insight into these stories so that we can begin to tackle the issue more heavily and demand the change that is needed for our future generations.

No one story is ever the same, but they all share similar themes.

Putting together this book, I found so many different stories that I wanted to put into words. I asked myself a lot about what I wanted this book to be. A story of one person or many? A story from my perspective or theirs? A story moving over time or a single moment? In the end, I decided I wanted this book to be like an album. I wanted each story to have its own rhythm and bridge and its own composer and theme like each song on an album. Then I wanted each story to work together so it could form a cohesive body of work. Ultimately, it didn't matter to me what I wanted this book to be like in the beginning but what I took away from writing it and putting these compilations of stories together in the end.

Women are strong and resilient. They have voices. We just need to provide them with the confidence to grow and use them.

Aryah.

A Growing Divide
Faisalabad, Pakistan

Sultana's Story

The screaming outcry of women and the high-pitched tears of children. The roaring of men and the clashing of silver. It's difficult to forget the noises my whole family and I heard when we had to move from India to Pakistan during the partition. I was only eight years old at the time, but some things are scarred in your brain.

It was a hard move. Everywhere you looked people were abandoning their prized possessions – their homes, their valuables – even some of their own family members. A lot was lost in the partition. Some people watched others being killed and some watched goods being stolen. The partition allowed old men to dream up a war for young men to fight. Everyone felt that they had to support one country or the other and in the process, many people lost their humanity.

The saddest part of the partition was seeing your neighbours become strangers – for me, it was anyway. Overnight, life turned into chaos. Invisible border lines divided people who had been friends for years. We were having to choose sides. Choose faiths. Choose our identities.

When we lived in India, we were wealthy. We lived comfortably. When we arrived in Pakistan, we had almost nothing. I lost my little sister Farhana in the move over and had we started our journey one train later, we'd probably lost our own lives too. The partition changed our lives as we knew it, but we made the best that we could of the situation – after all, this was our new life now. Of course, we missed our family that we parted from as we migrated. We lived in a joint family system in India and now we all lived scattered in different homes but at least we were all still here. We got to move on with our lives. We had the chance to try and find humanity in ourselves once again.

My father was very clever. He was a lawyer and fortunately, your national identity didn't change your brain ability. He worked extremely hard to rebuild our lives in Pakistan and we quickly regained the monetary wealth we had lost. The money could not substitute some of the sentimental possessions we had left behind like some of the cross-stitch artwork my Nani had handmade or old family photos, but it was a start.

There were some things the partition could never take away from me.

It didn't matter whether we were in India or Pakistan, my goals stayed the same. I wanted to study. My dad was very supportive of this. However, as one of seven sisters and one brother, my mum didn't want me to continue to study further. My elder brother and sister were both married, and my mother was watching her younger daughters begin to get proposals and start their married lives elsewhere. For my mother, there was a slight pain and a larger irritation, seeing her second eldest daughter ageing away. It was clear that a lot of the pressure she gave me was because of society, but I didn't care.

I was stubborn.

Life was not going to be dictated to me by other people. My father fully supported me, and I went to college. I studied sewing, textiles, and art. I was a very hands-on person and really enjoyed my course.

My stubbornness and disdain for marriage annoyed my mother. She was tired of hearing the word 'no' come out of my mouth. We had many proposals come to our house and no matter how much I pleaded that I was not interested, my mum was convinced that once I met them, I would change my mind. I played up every time someone came to visit, and this only pushed my mum further towards the edge – but my father found it very amusing.

At the age of twenty-one, I completed my education and looked forward to the next chapter of my life as a working woman. However, my mum continued to try and guilt me into marriage. Social pressure continued to mount, and my mum kept saying, "Sultana why don't you understand that you are getting too old, and no one will want you."

My mum was having my last sister at the time. Although the money wasn't an issue for my dad, the mounting pressure and endless conversation led me to relieve him of his fatherly duty. He kept getting an ear-bashing from my mother every time he supported me in my decision, so I thought now was the time to finally move forward. I had no interest in marriage, but it was the right thing to do for our family.

I only saw the man I had married on my wedding night. That was how most marriages were done then. I don't think I minded too much considering I wasn't even remotely interested in the union. I just told my mum to ensure that he was kind. Looks and anything beyond that did not matter to me. His family lived not too far from mine. Once I was married, I moved in with his family and that's when life really began to change.

Married life was not what I thought it would be. My husband was a good man, but my in-laws were not. My mother-in-law was very difficult. Nothing I did was good enough for her. I was constantly put down and if my husband tried to stand up for me, she would put me down even more for turning a son on his own mother. My father-in-law was not much better. He had a superiority complex. My dad and father-in-law had many problems after my marriage. My dad was no one's fool, and my father-in-law didn't like being anyone's equivalent. He used to get back at my dad by making my life difficult.

There was a time in my marriage when my husband and I were kept separate. I remember going days without seeing him. My husband came up with his own little plan to see me, passing notes through his younger brother. I used to give my brother-in-law the shopping list in the morning. Shopping for household groceries was the only time I was allowed to leave the house. My husband would get everything and hide it outside the house. When I would leave to do the shopping that day, I would meet my husband at the end of the road and an hour with him. We'd go out to eat ice cream or have a cup of tea away from the family. We felt like two criminals sneaking in the dark of the night, but we weren't doing anything wrong. When I got back, I would walk in with the shopping that had been left hidden for me.

As hard as life got, I never spoke back to my in-laws. I never tried to challenge them. It wasn't worth it because they would just find other ways to lash out at us. I knew from the beginning of my marriage that my husband and his father had a difficult relationship. There were often times my husband would work all day at one of the factories his family-owned. It was really tiring work and he would come home drained but happy with the money he had made. My father-in-law would come into our room after dinner and take his earnings for the day – leaving us with just enough to live on for the week.

My husband spoke a lot about escaping his family home. He dreamed of much more. He knew we were both capable people. I wasn't worried about where I lived. I was realistic and made the best of whatever situation I was in. I had to be sensible for both of us. We lived with his family for two years and everything seemed to become harder. The idea of escaping felt like a distant dream but after the birth of our first son, my husband knew we could not betray our future anymore. One day he said to me, "Sultana, I need you to trust me. I'm going to get us out of here. I promise that as soon as I can, I will call for you."

My husband left in January – our son was only two months old, to find our chance in the world. I left his family home eleven months later after great hardship. I moved to England with my baby boy and met my husband at Heathrow Airport.

We hoped that England would provide us with the opportunities that we could not have for ourselves back in Pakistan.

A Coffee...with a Side of Cancer, Please?
Utrecht, Netherlands

Margot's Story

This coffee shop is a haven. I come in here every morning. Sometimes just for ten minutes and other days for hours.

"What is Margot going to do next?"

That was what I asked myself every day as I inhaled my first whiff of fruity coffee beans in the morning. I've thought a lot about my life here. About how much has happened from the moment I stepped into this shop and ordered my first coffee. About how much can still happen.

Five years ago, I was diagnosed with stage four breast cancer. It was touch and go for months whilst doctors decided what type of treatment to do. I spent a lot of time researching the words they'd used during my consultation – often searching on my phone whilst they'd leave the room for a few minutes. I didn't really know what was actually happening. It was a continuous cycle of people asking me, "Margot, what do you want to do?" or "Margot, do you think this would be an option for you?" and I was just crumbling inside. One day I was deciding whether to follow my husband Tom on an American adventure and now I had to decide if I wanted to try and live. I mean *really* live.

In the end, I decided to go ahead with chemo, radiation, and a mastectomy. I was a fighter after all. However, no one can prepare you for a boxing fight with cancer. I'd never felt so tired in my entire life. Cancer didn't just throw me off physically. It made me really, really sad. It messed with my emotions. My doctors encouraged me to think positively during my chemotherapy, radiation and mastectomy but for a long time after my mastectomy, I really felt like I lost a piece of myself. I tried to write a book during my chemotherapy sessions, but my notepad was just filled with tear stains. Every word I thought. Every story that came to mind. Tom tried to be my 'chemo buddy' but he was just as lost and confused as I was. He didn't know the right words to say (I don't think anyone did) and even when he did say something right, he just had this look of pity and sorrow on his face every time he saw them stick another needle in me or take me for another test.

Everything was just so sad but sad felt like too simple a word to describe my emotions. I kept thinking I was going to die. When my hands started shaking, around my second round, I knew I couldn't write anything. It just made me feel like I was failing. I had the full support of my husband but that never felt like it was enough.

I never felt like enough anymore.

I had this spark to life before I was diagnosed. I had all these options, but the cancer diagnosis felt like a stop sign and the treatment kicked me even harder. I lost all my enthusiasm. I lost my positivity.

Before cancer happened, I had a lot of ambition. I had been thinking of starting a business or maybe writing children's stories. I'd always been creative as a child – my mind bursting with thoughts, but the ideas never really came to fruition. I thought that now was maybe the time. My husband would be travelling for work, and I thought I could go with Tom. I had no real job and we had nobody but ourselves to worry about. It seemed like I could accomplish anything if only I put my mind and time to it but that all disappeared after cancer. I got much more self-conscious. I started to think, *If bad things can happen at any time – why even bother?*

I'm so glad I didn't give up though.

Between the treatments, I was near tears every day. I was scared of just going to sleep because I thought I might die but I've now decided cancer was a blessing. I now knew what it felt like to think you've made mistakes in life like you wasted your time on trivial decisions and always planning for later. That you were going to die having not achieved your goals. Your dreams. Cancer made me want to live every day to the fullest.

During my entire cancer treatment, I was upset because I felt like Margot had died. I had lost so much of myself that it didn't feel like I was really alive anymore. How was I going to live on if I was already dead? However, now I know that *that* Margot did die, and it was a refreshing rebirth for me.

I've been in remission for three years now. I go for regular checks but thankfully, everything's been okay. I started working last year in an office, but I left it after a couple of months. It didn't feel right, and I decided I didn't have the time to waste on something that wasn't making me happy. I'm back in my local coffee shop and watching the men work on the building across the road whilst I drink my coffee. They're working on my coffee shop except mine's going to have lots of books in it. A library and a bookshop. I mean, why can't I combine my love of coffee and books…oh and cake. Lots of cake.

Tom and I are also on the adoption list. We're waiting for them to get my last set of scans before they finally sign us off and start trying to find us a child. After my treatment, I decided I needed to help another life after my own had been saved. I'm not a religious person but I felt like I had been given a mission to complete. I'm looking forward to balancing a child in the midst of all my new beginnings.

I've still got a lot more to do though. I'd love to write books and stories for children. I think that's the next thing on my to-do list. For now, though, I'm happy with beating cancer and opening my own business but when I get my child, I'm sure they'll inspire me to move on to my next chapter. Maybe they'll even be my first critic.

Stopping the Violence
Manila, Philippines

Abela's Story

I'm starting a support group at my university to break the stigma around domestic violence.

My goal is to try and give women confidence. To try and create a safe space for people to talk about the things you only hear in whispers or through silent messages. I want to break the taboo around domestic violence. I know what it's like.

When I was younger, I lived under the dictatorship of my father. He was a cruel man. He'd throw things. He'd punch us. My father didn't care what he hit when he was in one of his moods. We had a lot of restrictions on us. My dad would always pick me up from school and drop me off. He didn't trust that I wouldn't go somewhere else or with someone else. We weren't allowed to go out on the weekends or weeknights. Friends' houses were a definite no and birthday parties were practically a sin. Everything was watched. From my looks to my education. I wasn't allowed to wear makeup or perfume. I wasn't allowed to take part in my art classes. I wasn't allowed to study anything that allowed my mind to be free. We didn't even have our bedroom doors because he thought we'd try and do something. There were days I would get beaten up for wearing my skirt just above my ankles. My father would call me a 'slut' for talking to a male teacher. I was constantly put down for things that were out of my control. I would be punished for them too.

It was my sister, my mum and me. None of us were safe although I would often take the brunt of the beatings for my little sister. She was so fragile. She would just start shaking every time she heard the front door open. For a long time, she became mute because she was so afraid of saying the wrong thing. My sister thought it was better to say nothing but even that wasn't enough.

I had to do so many little things to help us survive.

I told the nuns at my school. I told our neighbours to call the police if they heard screaming. I made a duplicate key so we could go back for food whenever we escaped the house. My father was a very aggressive man.

During one argument, I remember I tried to put myself between him and my mother. It was probably the most aggressive I'd ever seen him get with her. There was blood everywhere. Her eye had been punched so much that she couldn't open it. Her arms were black and bruised as she had tried to use them as a shield, and I could hear her bones cracking. I couldn't watch it anymore, so I stepped in to try and stop him. He grabbed a knife off the kitchen counter and held it to my throat for the longest four minutes of my life. I remember him saying, "Abela, you're a disgrace to me," and "I never wanted you, Abela," and "You make my life harder – you're a living hell."

I was petrified, but I'd been terrified for most of my life, so I knew exactly what I was going to do.

The only thing I could do that night was remove myself from the situation. When my dad left for his weekly poker game, he bolted our front door shut. I walked over to help my mum, who was sitting as comfortably as she could on the floor. There wasn't much I could do to ease the pain for her because a lot of her bones had been broken. I didn't understand why my mum had put up with my father. I was fourteen years old and all I could remember was living under his reign. I knew that death was a one-time experience and if I did not leave, my father would somehow ensure that mine would be soon.

I asked my mother to move away with me. I already had all our bags packed but she couldn't do it. She said, "Abela, my sweet girl, I cannot leave him." He still had a hold over her.

I refused to stay in the toxic environment anymore. I couldn't do it. I wasn't strong enough. I prayed for my mother and planted a kiss on her forehead. I grabbed my little sister and told my mum I was taking her with me. She pleaded that I leave her behind and I felt ashamed for making my mother have to beg at my feet, but I couldn't leave my sister. I had to save what was left of her.

It was at the church that night that I watched my sister sleep the best sleep she had for years. I kept fidgeting with my watch. The hands of time moved faster and faster as it expected me to rush into our next step. I couldn't sleep. I panicked; I didn't know where we'd go. We had to move far away from here because otherwise, he'd find a way to make us go back. He always found a way and I think that's what made us so scared to leave before. I didn't want to move too far though just in case my mum changes her mind. I tried to reflect on my life. I remember feeling happy because I'd been alive for fourteen years, and I'd protected my mother for all that time. I felt like a failure though for not being able to carry her over that final hurdle. I kept picturing what my father was going to do to her now that we'd left but I couldn't go back. No matter how bad my head told me it was going to be for her.

It was one of the priests in the early morning who came up to me first. Gently waking me up from the wooden bench we had fallen asleep on, he told me he had to take me somewhere. I begged him not to take us home. I told him how bad my dad was and that I had to save my sister. I needed to give her some sort of future. He told me to trust him, and I had no choice but to.

We ended up in a hospital room an hour later. My mum was bandaged almost everywhere but she was sitting on the bed with her jacket on and her bag by her foot. I don't know what happened that night after we left but she said she was ready to start living for her girls.

We've been sober of him for nearly five years. We don't look over our shoulders when we speak to people. We don't flinch when the door opens or closes. We don't live in a fear of breaking physically or mentally.

We have about seventy members so far for my support group at my university to break the stigma around domestic violence but we're growing every day. My sister is actually going to give a speech at our church tomorrow to try and get more support from our local churches.

I set this group up to help break the taboo of domestic violence but really, I'm just hoping this group gives more women or girls the courage to change their own futures. Even if it's just one.

Ms Flores
Los Angles, USA

Summer's Story

When did everything change for me? That's an easy question. When I met Ms Flores.

Throughout school, I loved debate and discussion. I joined my leadership team in fourth grade and carried on through the fifth. At the end of fifth grade, we were meant to take a team trip to Washing DC to see where all the action took place. Our fifth-grade group put in the effort. We didn't want to let anyone down. We held fundraisers and everything – we even went as far as selling cookies door to door. We had all the funding sorted but when it was time to go, I didn't have the identification papers to get on a plane. I felt like I was letting the team down when everyone said they wouldn't go if I couldn't go. I knew everyone else dreamed of seeing the sights just as much as me. Ms Flores found me at the end of the school day and said, "Summer, don't worry about it. Just come on Monday with a bag packed."

Our teacher Ms Flores decided that if we couldn't get a plane, we'd all take a bus ride there. Just so I could go too. That trip changed my life. It wasn't the sights or the politicians that we met. It was Ms Flores's kindness. It made me want to be a lawyer. I didn't want anyone to be held back because of where they came from – just like Ms Flores didn't want it to stop me from going to Washington. After that day, Ms Flores became one of the closest people in my life.

We always kept in touch with one another after I left school. She basically watched me grow up. I had a lot of problems growing up. My mum was bipolar, and my dad couldn't get a visa to the States from Venezuela. There was this one time in high school I got in a huge fight with my mum when she was having an episode. I tried to calm her down, but she punched me in the stomach before kicking me out the front door. Ms Flores came and took me on a long car ride. I started to tell her everything. I told her about my mum and how she's been getting worse. I told her about the problems with her medical care and how we were struggling to get her to see the right doctor. I told her about a recent break-up and how I smoked weed. I told her about how 'I did this' and 'I did that'. She just listened to everything and kept repeating, "Everything's going to work out just fine for you, Summer."

Then Ms Flores started telling me about her life too. She told me that she'd been in an abusive relationship and had to go into protection. She told me about how one day she had all her friends, a home and a steady job and the next she'd been moved to a place where she knew no one and hadn't ever been before. I'd always thought her life was perfect because she was always smiling. She was a guidance counsellor, and she gave the best advice. I never thought about what she'd been through. I never even contemplated that she'd been damaged in some way too.

Ms Flores had been through so much, but she was probably the happiest and most caring person I knew – nothing could take the smile off her face.

When it came around to the time that college applications were due, Ms Flores was the one who helped me. I thought she'd laugh at me when I told her I wanted to apply to become a lawyer and work for DACA, but instead, she told me about the TheDream.us scholarship. I initially thought being a lawyer was just another dream that I couldn't make come true. I was ready to give it up. I'd kind of just accepted that I'd always work in restaurants like my mum – after all my grades weren't great for a scholarship and I couldn't afford college any other way. Ms Flores made me apply. She said, "what happened to that girl who wanted to be a lawyer?"

I learned that I got the scholarship that February. They paid for my entire college tuition and housing. Ms Flores was so proud of me. She kept saying, "I told you so, Summer."

I'm busy working as a trainee at an immigration firm at the moment, but in my spare time, I always stop and think that none of this would be happening without her. Without Ms Flores.

My Mother's Teachings
Jakarta, Indonesia

Chenda's Story

Mum raised me on her own since I was young.

My dad didn't care about our family. He was there physically, but he wasn't there in any other way. He didn't want to be a parent – he was certainly no father to me. My dad kept all his income for himself. Every last penny. If we brought anything for the house, he would gamble away our possessions. We were scared to buy ourselves anything. He would just end up selling it. He sold our jewellery. He sold our electronics. He even sold our furniture.

Somehow my mother still did everything for him. She cooked his food, did his washing, ironed his clothes…everything. She had to work as a housemaid around the hours she knew he wouldn't be home. He never supported her in any way financially, but if she tried to work herself, he would scream and take her money away from her. My mum used to hide her earnings in the pole of my metal bed. My dad would check underneath my mattress every day after he came back from wherever he had been, but never the frame.

I think my mum stuck around because of how she was raised. People talked about you all the time and you became a woman with a scarlet letter in our community if you leave your husband – even if it's his fault and everyone knows it.

I asked my mum time and time again why we had to stay. I told her about the stuff I read in books and saw on the TVs on my way home. I told her we could do so much better. She always rebuffed me though – "Chenda, this is our little corner of the world, and we have to learn to make it flower here." My mother kept saying that we have to be kind – even to those that have wronged us, for we do not know what battle they are fighting that day.

Then one day when Mum came home from work and I came back from school, the house was empty. There was nothing left. Our furniture. Our cooker. Everything was gone but a few of our clothes. My mum spent the whole evening trying to work out how much money she had so she could replace everything. She refused to stop making lists and working out costs. She kept telling me about how "Auntie down the road had an old sofa out in front of her house on Monday. Maybe we could ask her if we could have it, Chenda." It was midnight when I put her pen down and told her it was time to go.

My mum cried for the rest of the night whilst I packed away what was left of our clothes into some plastic shopping bags I got from my neighbours.

After that night we moved as far away from our town as possible. I didn't want my mum to have to be reminded of him or forced to listen to what people would say. For the last two years, we've been living in a rented house together. My mum seems so much happier now – like her broken back has been fixed. We can own our own things now without fear of losing them. We can actually make progress and move forward in life. That kind of change has been good for us both.

I've started working at a pharmacy recently so that I can pay my way through university.

My mum raised me well by herself. A few months back, I decided to get back in touch with my father. He's lost his job but still manages to find something to gamble. I give him enough money for rent and food but refuse to let him know where we now live.

I have no interest in taking revenge. I'm showing him how he should have treated us. I don't have to live that life again, but I don't need to be bitter about it either.

Sorry

Cape Town, South Africa

I know girls who spill 'I'm sorry' from their mouths like they pump blood into their veins. Others walk into them or shout at them and yet they still stutter an apology out of fear of doing something wrong – when they have done anything at all to apologise for.

Sometimes, I am one.

I know girls who apologise for asking to go to the bathroom during their lessons, who apologise for everything because they feel like they are taking up more than their fair share of space on this planet.

Sometimes, I am one. Everything starts with an 'I'm sorry' (and ends with one too) – constant bookends that we don't even notice anymore. We delete her apology the way we delete likes and um's from speeches.

Sometimes, I am one.

I know girls with ten times more apologies than misdemeanours and wonder how often they hear 'it's okay'.

Sometimes, I am one.

You are more than okay. You do not need to apologise for being here. For being yourself.

Homeless

Manchester, England

Abbey's Story

Growing up in the foster system, I was seriously let down by social services. I was a vulnerable girl, exposed from all angles.

The problem with the social system is that, if you're a baby and adopted you're almost assured to have a great life – although I've seen first-hand that that is not always the case. However, if you're older, your chances of being adopted decrease every day. Eventually, you're moved from home to home with no stability. Each house is different with different people. Not everyone is nice or safe.

Relationships for me were difficult. I had a lot of trust issues because of my life in the system. I was abandoned by my parents. I was abandoned by a lot of people in the various houses I stayed. Friends quickly disappeared and when it came to the chance of being adopted, even those who you thought would help you would turn. I didn't know how to act in a relationship or what a healthy relationship was because I was abused so much by the men and women in my life – some selling me out and others taking me for themselves.

It made it difficult for me. I was always lonely.

Turning eighteen, I was a healthy, single girl who needed a home. I went to the council for assistance. Many people kept telling me that the council could help me, so I went but even they refused. They said they couldn't assist me because I couldn't be given 'priority need'. I was healthy and fine. I needed to find a home for myself. However, I was broke and had no current prospect of getting a job. With no money and no one to vouch for me, I ended up being homeless and sleeping rough on the streets.

The streets were brutal. I had no way of escaping them. I had no education to get a job and no money to go anywhere else. I was still deemed healthy and single, so the council was still not an option.

Being on the streets, I learnt what it meant when people said it was survival of the fittest. The first few nights of sleeping rough were hard but it was probably the easiest my life was going to be for a while. I remember the first night someone picked me up. It was freezing. Cars were iced over and the bench I was hiding behind, smelt of rotting wood as the cold wind froze the water on it. He just picked me up off the ground. No words. No questions. Just picked me up and threw me into the back of his car. He got on top of me, and I didn't have any way of stopping him. I screamed but there was no one around to hear me. No one cared enough to check what was going on. I closed my eyes and kept saying to myself, "Abbey this is a bad nightmare, you'll wake up." It wouldn't stop though. When it did, he threw me out onto the dark, cold pavement next to his car. A couple of monetary notes were thrown onto me as he drove away. I was paralysed from the pain. Everything hurt so much that I couldn't even walk properly. I can't forget the smell of strong vodka mixed with cigarettes that wrecked from his skin. The bloodshot redness of his eyes as he forced himself into me. He didn't care. I was a piece of lifeless meat to him.

The next night I hid behind a different tree, miles away from that spot. I don't know how I managed to walk that far. I was shaking from pain – grasping onto anything I could to help me move. My body was bruised all around my upper thighs. I was bleeding from everywhere he had attacked me, but I had no resources to buy anything to help and a hospital was too far away for me to make it there conscious. I had bitten bruises around my neck. Whenever I walked past someone and they saw them, they gave me this look. Like it was my fault. It riddled me with shame. Like I should have been stronger or wiser.

The nightmare wasn't over then though. He found me somehow and it happened all over again. And again. And again.

During one of the days after he left, a woman came up to me and tried to give me a small pack of white powder. I refused profusely. I didn't want to try it and I knew I certainly couldn't afford to keep up the habit. She asked me my name and I muttered it out in shame. Did I even want people to know that this is what Abbey had become? I was ashamed I couldn't erase it from my own head. She pushed the small packet into my hand. "Abbey, you'll want this. It will help make you forget. This one's on me."

After he left me that night, I had the whole packet. The first hit couldn't make me forget. Neither could the second. Eventually, I did through, until it started all over again and I was desperate for another hit. Then there were others who did the same. Who watched him finish with me, throw me out of his car and would then just scoop me up from the floor and start the cycle all over again. The more it happened the more I needed to escape. There was no stopping these people. I tried so hard to push them off me, but they were animals. Barbaric animals who would push their fat, dirty skin against mine and crush me under their weight.

I had given up the fight.

It took a few months before I became completely lost to myself. Abbey was so far from my mind. She no longer existed. She had been broken, bruised and left to die. The drugs were mixed with alcohol. I was someone else. I stopped trying to fight it because there was nothing to gain. They would not stop. They would not leave me alone. I was a toy to be passed around and as they did, I just counted down until my next hit.

Eventually, I wised up. I knew I could survive if I played it smart. I needed the drugs to function. These men would not leave me alone and more kept coming out of the woodwork. So I took back the power. I made the decisions. I was in the winter of my life. I fell asleep in a new place almost every night with visions of myself dancing, crying and laughing with them. The drugs distorted my trust and my mind. These people would be abusing me, but they provided me warmth and comfort for the night and in the morning, they gave me enough money to get my next hit. They provided me with one less night on the cold streets, starving and penniless.

For three years, my life felt like I was on an endless world tour. My memories of those warm moments were the only thing that sustained me during the time. It sounded weird but with all the drugs in my system, those men provided me with a safety that was not afforded to single women on the streets. On paper, all you can see is that they paid me with money and drugs but at the time it felt different. After the first few months of having no choice, I now decided where I would spend the night and who I would spend it with. Some of these men paid me with memories of laughter and happiness that I could not get anywhere else. These were the only relationships I could afford myself to have. There was little attachment but a vulnerability every night from them. Some brought me to share their secrets with a stranger they knew they would never see again. For me, it was different though. In all the drug-fuelled moments I had, the contact they made and their money, provided me with a way to move forward. To forget about the coldness in my heart and the winds that ran across me on the rough pavement streets.

In the few moments I was sober and clean, I wished over and over again for change but in the end, I had no choice but to not mind. I knew I didn't have any prospects besides this, so this was what I would have. When some people I used to know found out what I was doing, how I had been living, they asked me why. They wanted to know so much but there's no use in talking to people who have a home, who have already made up their mind about you. They have no idea what it's like to sink your future and safety into other people's hands. To think that if you could choose which buyer gets you, you can control the amount of pain they will inflict on you that night. For home to be wherever you can lay your head. To belong to no one. To everyone.

Every night I used to pray that I'd find my people. That I'd find myself. Eventually, I did.

One night, a man approached. He rambled on about something, but I was too high to understand. I did understand when he said, "do you want to come with me?" I assumed now would be the time I follow him to the back of a car or some greasy hotel room and take my clothes off for him. I followed willingly. I don't remember what happened but when I woke up, I found myself sleeping on a fold-out bed in the middle of a large hall. A thin but warm blanket covered me, and I had a soft pillow to rest my head on. A small plate of bread sat next to me. I remember that being the best bread I had eaten in years. I didn't know any of the people there but they were all kind to me.

I left that morning and didn't return to that warm place that night. It felt like a dream being there. Like the drugs were playing with my mind. After a few days on the streets, I found myself walking back to the centre. No street corner to lay my head on, no money and clothes that were extremely worn. My memories were blurred, and I was shaking as I hadn't had a hit in a few days and was suffering from withdrawal, but the place was still as warm as I remembered.

The people took one look at me, and I thought they would send me away. I smell and looked dirty, but they surprised me. They pulled me into the warm, large hall and gave me a bed for the night. In the morning they brought me a fresh pair of clothes, they were a little big but the lady that gave them to me insisted they'd keep me warmer than what I was wearing. That night, I spent my time among people that were homeless, and addicts like me. It was a wake-up call for me. I realised I needed to straighten myself out.

It took almost a year, I was still on the streets, but I became clean with the help of the centre. Any time I had a craving, I would go there, and they would give me a hot cup of tea and just talk to me. It was so comforting to have someone there. The kindness of strangers.

After a month of coming and going to the centre, I asked if I could help out in anyway. I watched what they did every day, and I knew these people that walked in better than they did. I was one of them, so they let me help out as a volunteer at the centre. They didn't pay me with money, but they paid me in kind for my help. They didn't realise how much it was actually them, helping me. During the year I was a volunteer, they helped me improve my reading and my writing during the long but quiet night shifts. They helped me learn how to use computers and technology. They helped me rebuild my life. They provided me with a summer to escape the winters of my life.

Now I work with homeless charities full time. I'm on a proper pay and I feel so fulfilled all the time. I found the Abbey I had lost and combined her with the strength I had gained in the years she had gone. Every time I see someone like me walk into any of the centres or on any of the streets, I stop and talk to them. I learn how I can help them. Sometimes, it's the conversation that changes everything for them.

It took me seven years to get to where I am today, but I have finally found myself. My people. My calling.

His Death Ruined Me
Karachi, Pakistan

Nilam's Story

I came from a very traditional family. I had a very sheltered childhood. I stayed home and only went to school. My friends would always come to my house. My life revolved around household work or homework.

I went straight from my father's house to my husband's house. From being Nilam Abbas – daughter of Abbas Khan, to being Nilam Haider – wife of Haider Shah. My mother taught me the basics of homemaking. I learned to balance my home life with my education but eventually, something had to give, and I would not need any further education when my children came.

If I ever needed anything, my mother would ask my father to bring it on his way back from work or I would ask my husband – who would do the same. I learnt from my mother that my place was in the home. I was to be there and ready when my husband woke up in the morning or came home from work. I tried not to ask him for too much – I remember how my father reacted at times when my mother asked him for something she had forgotten to ask for previously from the shops. I did not want my husband to act the same way towards me. My mother told me, "Nilam, you should not put him out after a long day's work," and that it was her fault when he shouted at her. She should have been more considerate. That's what my mother taught me. I needed to be considerate of my family but most importantly, my husband's needs.

I got a basic education. When I was growing up, a girl's position was to be seen as a homemaker and nothing more. By the age of eleven, my mother had taught me to make many curries, rice and chapattis. All our guests always said I'd be an excellent wife one day. My father didn't see it as necessary for me to carry on with my education after my SSC. With an SSC I would get a good husband.

My husband passed away eight years ago. We had been together for over twenty years. His death ruined my life.

I had never been prepared for what happens when the head of the household passes away. My mother, father and husband all never prepared me. My husband took care of all our finances. He worked and paid for our bills. He brought our shopping. I was so dependent on him that I didn't even realise it. I couldn't do anything for myself.

I couldn't pay my rent anymore. I couldn't feed myself. The people in the neighbourhood tried to help me at first. My husband was a good man and very respected in our neighbourhood so after he passed, people wanted to help me the best way they could. Every day they would arrange two or three hundred rupees to pay my bills and send groceries to my house. I sold everything I could to try and pay for myself. Most of my jewellery, furniture and clothes. People saw that I was trying to support myself and helped me for as long as they could. Like everything though, eventually, their charity ran out. I understood. They had families to support and many of them did not earn that much. They told me it was time to seek help from God as they could no longer help.

My husband should have been more considerate. He should have known that I would have nothing without him. He should have taught me to know more. Maybe he was afraid I would talk out against him if I knew more but that doesn't excuse the situation, he has left me in.

Now I sleep on the floor of a relative's house – moving from house to house when one tires of me. I help out where I can – looking after their children or helping with household work but I am not as young as I used to be. During my free days, I sit and beg to pass the time. With the money I have saved, I have started to look for work. Someone helped me put together my skills and I am going to start sewing clothes for women in my neighbourhood in a few weeks. It's hard work, but for me it is manageable. I'm just waiting to get my sewing machine this Friday. Friday is a good day for a new beginning.

This is the fate God has chosen for me. When I talk about these things, my heart begins to sink. I push these thoughts out of my head and stay quiet. If I don't think about my feelings, I feel okay.

I no longer go by Nilam Haider. I didn't revert back to Nilam Abbas either. As much as these men in my life loved me, they failed to teach me to stand on my own. To be prepared for the worse. A woman is very strong and adaptable but only if you give her the wings to learn to fly first. The hardships I have struggled with since they both passed have been harder than anything else I have ever faced in life because I was not given the chance to learn. Leaving home and getting married to a stranger. Trusting we'd have enough money every week when my husband first started working for a small company. My three miscarriages. Nothing has been worse than being left to rot on my own. I now go by Nilam Zahra. When I heard that Zahra meant flower, I knew I wanted it to be my name. I may be old but just like a strong-rooted plant learns to flower in the spring, I too shall find my way to flourish once again.

In the Air
Algiers, Algeria

Wafaa's Story

At school, we were given the chance to shadow professionals in the workplace. I grew up poor so I knew I wanted a job where I could earn a good wage and get my mum and siblings out of the slums we lived in. We'd had to share a one-room, small hut for as long as I could remember. We had mattresses spread out over the floor and a small washing line to divide the room. We didn't have enough space for a kitchen, so our stove used to be outside, and the toilet was at the end of the quarter. We shared the single toilet with about fifteen other families that lived in the same conditions as us.

At the time I remember wanting to be a doctor. Everyone around me was always so sick and none of us could afford to go to the hospital or even buy basic medicines. I emailed a lot of hospitals to see if I could get some work experience, but I got no response. My teacher told me that the work experience was vital for my education and that a friend of hers worked in the back office of an airline company. She could get me the experience there if I wanted. I'd never flown on an aeroplane before and only saw them distantly in the sky. I didn't have any real interest in it, but I knew I wouldn't be able to find any better, so I agreed.

When I got there on my first day, I remember walking down the huge runway – planes all parked, and a few being moved and loaded. I spent all day in the office but when I was there, I just stared out the window. I couldn't believe how big they were – they looked so small whenever I saw them in the sky. Each one that landed mesmerised me. The lady I was working with could see that I wasn't interested in the paperwork, so she showed me the other side of the airport. The crew side. I couldn't even express how excited it made me. I was in awe of all of it. Whenever the pilots walked into the room, all I noticed was how incredible their posture was. All their hats were lined up on a shelf. Their jackets were all hanging in a row.

That's when the bug bit me.

I started spending all my holidays there and asked so many questions because my brain never stopped thinking. How do I do this? Where can I get that? When do we open this? I carried a notebook with me so I had all the information I could possibly write. I didn't want anything to stop me from achieving this goal. The pilots there were also so kind to me – I don't think they'd ever seen a girl so enthusiastic about becoming a pilot. They gave me advice and one even let me come on a short flight with them. It was the first time I'd ever been in an airplane and the first time I'd ever flown in one. I loved every second of it.

When I turned eighteen, there was nothing else I could think of doing besides becoming a pilot. I couldn't think of anything else in my future besides hearing this bubbling voice over the intercom saying, "Hello, this is your Captain Wafaa speaking." I visited a flight school that was near us and picked up three application forms – just in case I made a mistake on one of them. However, the costs were too much. I showed my mum the application with such excitement but when she saw how much the fees were, her face dropped, and she said we didn't have the money. She told me to apply to normal universities – she didn't want to stop my education, she just wanted me to aim for something more affordable. My mum would bring me applications for many local and cheaper universities, but I couldn't give up my dream like that. There was nothing I wanted more. I kept hiding the forms under my bed and telling her I got rejected. I found an internship with a glider company and used my pay to buy my first pilot's uniform. I put one stripe on the sleeve – for student. When I came home that night, I think that was the first time she (my mum) took me seriously. I don't know whether it was the uniform or the excitement in my eyes, but she could see her daughter really wanted to fly and nothing was going to stop me.

After my uniform, I didn't spend my internship money on anything else except for my university fees and books. My mum tried to help me pay for flight school, but we really struggled. Some months we had enough and other months we were barely surviving ourselves. It meant that I would have to drop out of university for a few weeks but because flying involves so much muscle memory, by the time I returned, it would take me a while to get back on track.

One day, I was waiting for my bus to come. I stood by the small stall next to my stop. I looked at all the magazines that hung around the stand – their glossy covers flooded from page to page with companies that had the money to make dreams happen. I bought a stack of magazines and newspapers. I went through every page and cut out the advertisements. I went to the local supermarket, and I wrote down every brand I could see. I sent all of them letters asking for help knowing that it might not work but that this was my best chance.

This was my lifeline.

Almost everyone said, "No but we wish you the best of luck, Wafaa." However, I did receive a small amount from a grocery shop and another brand sent me a brand-new watch with a letter suggesting that I do a raffle with it. That was a huge break. I sold seven hundred raffle tickets and from there, things were going so well. African Pilot Magazine promoted the raffle for free. A gentleman from England bought 100 tickets. I was earning enough money to begin paying for flight school again. However, when the lottery board saw my advert in the magazine, they sent me a letter saying that it was illegal for me to sell the tickets and to end my raffle immediately. I tried really hard to explain that I was raising money for my education, but they didn't seem to care. I had never felt so crushed in my life. I'd have to sit out another year of flight school and fall even further behind. I got out all the contact details for the people who had sent me money and began to call them to explain the situation and return their money like I had been told to do. Nobody would accept their money back. They told me to keep it and it was enough to keep me in the air for months.

It was getting to the end of five months and my mind started to hurt again. The money was running out and I would have to give up this thing I love because I couldn't think of any more ways to make the money. With Christmas of that year coming, I was defeated.

One of my mentors invited me to eat lunch at the airport and I accepted, wondering how I was going to tell them that now wasn't the right time for me to fly. I couldn't face the thought of having to admit that it was because we didn't have the money. They had sent a car to pick me up and I just couldn't put into words the disappointment I felt knowing there was nothing I could do to stop this dream from ending. When I stepped out of the car, everyone who had ever helped me was there. They all started clapping before somebody handed me the phone. A person on the other end said, "Hi Wafaa, you're on the line with the head of the studio and our network is going to pay for your entire education!" My heart dropped because I just couldn't believe it.

That was nearly four years ago now. I just got my license last week. I couldn't stop smiling every time I looked at it and saw 'First Captain Wafaa' written on it. I'm hoping to fly for Air Algérie, but there's still some more training I need to do before I'm a full-fledged Captain. I also want to do some teaching. I want to visit schools in poor neighbourhoods. Maybe save enough money to help another girl like me. I want all the kids to see what an African female pilot looks like. That if you work hard enough and try hard enough, nothing is a boundary.

The Story of My Headscarf
Washington DC, USA

Yasmin's Story

I was born in Baghdad, Iraq but we immigrated to Washington in 1982 after Iraq became politically dangerous. It was a long time before the 9/11 attacks, but the views people had against Muslims were starting to brew. They were beginning to hear the media really talk about Iraq, Muslims, and Islam and not in a flattering way. However, my parents saw the need for change in our lives and the move critical for our own safety.

When we got to America, my parents raised me very liberally. It was different from your stereotypical views of a Muslim and different to what I remember our lives to be in Iraq. I was given the freedom to mix with boys and go out clubbing with my friends but I didn't want that. The noise of the nightclubs gave me headaches and watching my friends drink themselves into oblivion did not appeal to me at all – especially as I watched people hit on my friends (both male and female) who were too out of their heads to defend themselves properly. It was the 'college' culture I had envisioned in my head when I watched all the American films, but it didn't feel like what I had imagined. It didn't live up to the expectations.

I think it's important to point out that my parents were liberal political thinkers. That's why Iraq was dangerous for us. My parents raised me on the belief that although every country has the authority to ensure order, we do not have to be suppressed by order. The government saw anything outside their regime as dangerous. I wasn't raised within a conforming environment. There was no glass ceiling because my Mama and Abu never said there was a limit. We were 'loose' Muslims – believing that we had to be kind and gentle with others so we could go to heaven or be punished in hell for our sins but that was it. We didn't pray or fast. There was no pressure to look like a Muslim. We simply had to be good people – and eat halal food (most of the time).

Due to this liberation from a young age, I always knew I wanted to use my voice to raise concern for issues that I saw as unfair or unjust. I used my voice in the playground when Dylan hit Safera on the head because she couldn't play with him – she wanted to play football, but Dylan said it wasn't a 'girls' sport. I used my voice again in middle school when my partner Robert expected me to do all the work with our pretend baby because I was a girl. All of these things felt like trivial matters until I used my voice again in high school when a group of white students tried to get our Arabic society shut down because they thought we were using it to spread a message of hate against the west – we were really just a small group set up to support foreign middle eastern students who had come over as refugees and needed help in communicating. We taught many people how to speak, read and write English – many of them got into college because of the support.

For me, that was a turning point. I wanted to use my voice within the blur of the media narrative of Muslims. I heard all these stories about the cruel acts happening in my homeland and how it was made more of a religious issue as opposed to a cruel dictatorship. After 9/11, the climate around Muslims became even more dangerous and the narrative even more violent. However, these people did not reflect any of the Muslims I knew. I knew Uncle Hashim who lived across the road. He and my father were extremely good friends, and he would send his daughter to walk me home from school if he ever saw me walking alone or come himself if he saw me being harassed. After 9/11, he brought a minibus so he could escort all the Muslim kids from my school home – hoping to prevent another one of us from being attacked, beaten or verbally abused. I knew Auntie Bushra who would make a weeks' worth of food for anyone who got a cold. After 9/11, she sent food to the homeless centre that was now holding people who had decided to move to Washington from New York. When she dropped it off the first time, she had her scarf pulled off her head, was spat at and told to go back to her own country – even though she was born and raised in Washington. However, that did not stop her. She continued to send the food, but she would just ask the white lady at the door to collect it from her car instead as she did not want to risk another incident or cause offence to anyone else.

These events in my life made it more important for me to know what being a young Muslim girl was. During my first year at university, I decided to wear a hijab. It was hard at first because I got so many racial slurs shouted at me. I lost friends because they couldn't get over their hatred for Muslims. I was still liberal in my religious thoughts and enjoyed the odd nights out with my friends but that didn't matter to people. I was still the same person but now all these people saw was my scarf and not my face. Yasmin was still Yasmin, but my friends saw 'covered' Yasmin as a danger. I got over it though because, for me, it was more important to learn my religion and be a positive representation amongst the midst of the media persona, than to have friends who weren't supportive or understanding.

Through my studies and journalism degree, I believe that being a young Muslim woman has always been seen as a critical agent of change. We've been needed to show this transformative movement between Islamic history in the Middle East and the modern westernisation of Islam. However, it's hard to be a Muslim woman these days because we've become symbols and not individuals. That's in no small part thanks to the global fixation on the headscarf. The western concept of a woman in a headscarf is very different to the individual identity they give to Western women. If you wear a headscarf anywhere in the Middle East or Asia, the west believes you must be devout, traditional, obedient, oppressed and conservative. There have been so many times I've been asked if I've been forced to wear my scarf or if I was told to wear a scarf because of my father or if I was a conservative Muslim because I came from Iraq. It frustrated me a lot because people thought I didn't have a brain of my own or my own strengths or even my own ideas of religion. A woman in her scarf is apparently nothing more than a religious person who follows a very rigid path of Islam. That's not me though and it's not most of the girls and women that I know.

It would be harsh of me to say that these assumptions made by non-Muslims are the only thoughts that exist. Upon a trip back to see my family in Iraq around 2006, I learned that the Middle East also allowed people to draw instant conclusions about your religious values if you were wearing a headscarf. A headscarf means you have set values in your beliefs.

A headscarf, it seems, is never just a headscarf.

In the end, I discovered that just like I wanted to wear my scarf to show a more positive view of my religion, other people also wanted their scarf to be an expression of some form. Many women in America continued to wear their scarves as a form of political expression and to cement their identity. To show 'I am a Muslim woman and proud to announce that through my physical adoption of the scarf'. Some women in the Middle East embraced their headscarves as part of a social pact with each other. "Let's all wear the same colour scarf on Wednesdays." This is no different from girls in America wearing the same sorority skirt as an expression of belonging to the same club – or wearing pink on Wednesdays. In places like Iraq, sometimes a headscarf is used as a security measure to avoid unwanted attention. The increased violence and terror over the last decade have prompted an increase in the number of women reaching for their headscarves. It was their way of distancing attention from themselves.

For me, the one thing that really prompted me to grab a headscarf was so I could be free. My parents were liberal, but I often felt their past tugging on their heartstrings. They would never dare ask me outright, but I knew them well enough to know it worried them. They wanted me to be somewhat religious, but they didn't want me to see religion as a confinement because Islam for us was actually a very liberal religion. The questions still swirled in their head. Was she really just going out with her friends? Did she have a boyfriend? Was she doing drugs?

When I put on a scarf there was a relaxation in my parents. Yes, some people in headscarves do have boyfriends and relationships outside of marriage and that is their choice, but for me, it acted as a warning sign. It stopped a lot of the harassment I got. The number of comments I got about how my ass looked in my jeans immediately dropped, and people thought twice before touching me in any way.

As a woman, I chose to wear a headscarf. There was no pressure and no conversation in my house about it. My own mother did not wear a headscarf and I think that had a lot to do with the way a headscarf was perceived in Iraq before she left. As a weapon to force on women. To hide and conceal women as a dirty secret. For my mother, a headscarf had been permanently chained to her memory as a pair of handcuffs, but I saw the scarf as a symbol. For my religion. For myself.

I work as a writer for a newspaper company in Washington now and I'm bombarded with questions that I try to answer in a weekly online forum called Yasmin Talks. Muslim women are still put into two categories. Headscarf equals religion. No headscarf equals secular. I'm working to change that. I wear my headscarf and I kept my fasts, but I often miss my prayers and fail on the other core values my religion instils. I know women who don't wear scarves but never miss a prayer or a religious lecture at the mosque. We must now work to find a balance. Each Muslim woman can choose her own practice of Islam. There are many ways to do so and for many, a scarf has no bearing on their decisions either way.

For me, wearing a scarf was a great decision. I've spent a lot of my life showing a positive side to a religion seen as a walking terror campaign. I've learnt about my religion, how to behave and how to follow it. Many people have seen that my religion is now beginning to be defined by the acts of many, not the few.

I'm working on changing people's perceptions. My scarf shows that the previous assumption that I only wear it because I'm oppressed is false. I'm campaigning on the streets. Waving signs outside of studios. Writing uncensored news articles. I work with all people to promote gender equality – both socially and religiously. I believe, that through active participation, we can help create a new way for modernism and Islam to coexist respectfully and peacefully for all. Not every story of a woman in a headscarf to be about devotion, tradition, obedience, oppression, conservatism, or terrorism, but about choice and the freedom for women to be able to make their own choice and be believed when they do.

My Father's Orchids and My Mother's Yellow Coronilla
Lima, Peru

Valentina's Story

My dad worked as a skipper on a fishing boat in Maine. He left us for eighteen months at a time. I saw him for maybe a month before he had to leave us again but the time I spent with him was epic. We didn't have much, but he would make paper turn into dreams. He built me castles, swans and aeroplanes with whatever we had around the house – cereal boxes, newspaper or envelopes. It was on his twelfth trip on a boat that caused a disaster. The boat turned on their last trip out to sea due to bad weather. We always knew there were risks with his work but after the fourth time he came back we all got comfortable. We thought it would never occur.

There were white orchids at his funeral along with yellow coronillas – my mum's favourite. He always said to bury him with a yellow coronilla so he could have a part of my mum with him. That was what I have been named after. A specific yellow shrub called coronilla Valentina's that had the most beautiful fragrance during the day. I dropped my favourite locket into his casket so that he could have a piece of me too.

It was hard growing up without my father. It was just me and my mum after he died. She worked really hard as a hotel maid but there was never enough money to cover the rent. We had to move in with my uncles when I was ten years old. There were twelve of us living in one house growing up. We had three bedrooms, one living room, a kitchen and a bathroom. We learnt to manage though.

My entire life I've watched people making sacrifices. Everyone in my house made a sacrifice for me. It was always, 'Valentina needs to have this' or 'Valentina must have that'. Two of my uncles put off getting married and moving out. My grandfather stopped going to his poker nights and retired a lot later than he should have. My grandmother gave up her Latina dance classes. My mum worked three jobs – in a restaurant, as a house cleaner and as a hotel maid. Everyone made sacrifices just so that I could go to university and so that I was never made to feel like I had less, just because I didn't have a father.

All my mum's money went towards my tuition. I remember one semester we were short on money. I told her I would just take a break until we had enough funds to send me, but she told me, "Don't worry about it, Valentina. I'll find it. You just continue." She's always been like that. She never wants me to be stressed or take on the burden of finances. She always told me to just focus on school.

Growing up, I often felt so guilty. Sometimes she would go to work with holes in the sole of her shoe, but she didn't care – she didn't want to waste money. I was only a child and easily brought any story my mum would tell me. I always trusted her completely. There were often times when there would only be enough food for one meal. By the time the meal was portioned into tiny sizes for her parents, her brothers and then I, there would be none left. My mum always said that she wasn't hungry. She would even give me her portion sometimes when she knew I had a bad day. She'd tell me she had an extra big lunch that day.

I didn't realise until I was older that she had only been pretending.

Finishing university was the biggest relief I ever felt. I knew I could finally start repaying everyone. No one expected me to but once I got a good job there was never a moment for me to take no as an answer. For three years I worked as a financial director for one of the largest banks in the country. The job let me make enough money to buy a large home for us all on the hill. My mum always wanted a house overlooking the water, so I brought her one that did exactly that. I've helped both my uncles get married and the other two find houses not too far – they both insisted it was time for them to move on now. I'm actually about to finish paying for their first daughter to finish university.

For the past five years, I've been trying to convince my mum to stop working. She had insisted on keeping her job as a hotel maid. Only recently have I been able to reach a compromise. We've just converted our old house into a centre for struggling women. My job was great, but I always felt empty when I got my paycheck. Now that all my debts had been paid, I wanted to give back and help other women in similar situations. My mum has agreed to run the centre for me.

She's never said anything about how she feels working there but I know she gets the same feeling that I do. Especially when our weekly order of white orchids and yellow coronillas arrives.

And Then It All Stopped
Amman, Jordan

Raniya's Story

I loved primary school. I had the most brilliant teacher. She was my role model. The way she taught me. The excitement and passion she had about sharing her knowledge. There was a real aurora about her. I don't remember deciding to be a teacher so much as remembering that I wanted to be just like her.

My whole life became about studying. I didn't want anything to stop me. I would ask for more work and topics that we would be learning next. I'd learn every lesson early so that I could participate in class and ask questions. I wanted to absorb as much knowledge as humanly possible.

Whilst my siblings were playing games around the house and outside running around with their friends, I'd put my earplugs in and work on my homework. My mum said it became an unhealthy obsession, but education was my passion. It was all I thought about. I didn't even want to get married – I didn't want that distraction. My desire to learn led me to finish at the top of my class in both high school and university. I wanted to study for my master's and applied to five different universities. I got a scholarship to pursue my masters in London and I took it.

It was whilst I was preparing to move to London that I met a man who was very supportive of me going to school. He loved my ambition and we shared similar interests and ideas. I decided to get married to him after he asked my father for my hand in marriage and after our wedding, we moved to London. Four months later he was killed in a car accident. I was two months pregnant.

I knew immediately after my husband's death that I would have to let go of my dreams. There was no way I could raise a child by myself in a foreign country with no support. I fell into a deep depression. I was going to be a single mother. I'd have to focus everything on raising my child, so they didn't feel neglected. It wasn't a concept in Damascus for a mother to raise a baby and work at the same time, let alone for a single mother to even dream it. It was too western a concept for women to have it all.

I thought that I would never be able to do anything in my life again. I skipped the orientation for the London University and got on a plane back to Syria. I gave birth to my daughter and moved in with my parents so that I could have help raising her. When I saw my daughter, I realised I needed to get my life back on track. She'd already lost a father. I didn't want her to have a hollow for a mother too.

I enrolled at the University of Damascus and continued with my dream to get a master's. I was working whilst studying. I moved out of my parent's house into a small apartment just down the road from them. They looked after my daughter on the days she did not have nursey whilst I was at work or university. I graduated once again at the top of my class, and I couldn't have been prouder of myself for doing so. I began to work as a professor while I applied for my PhD. I felt a little tingle in my stomach any time someone called me Professor Raniya. I could imagine my husband smiling at me with such joy because we had both thought about it often. My daughter was getting older and I was able to support her all by myself. Everything seemed to be getting back on track.

Then the war came.

Now that I'm a refugee, my life feels like it is always on pause. My studies have completely stopped. I'm not working because I don't have the right paperwork. I don't have a career. I'm a Syrian refugee and because of it, I'm not allowed to participate in society. I used to be a cheerful person. Now I like to be alone. I've become more nervous and aggressive.

The waiting was the worst part. You don't know when or where you're going to go. Most importantly I just want to finish my education, but mostly I just pray that whatever is waiting for me is better than what I've gone through.

I learnt last Tuesday that the professor position I had applied for in London a while back has been accepted and my paperwork should be finalised within the next two weeks. My daughter is very excited. We both know a little English but we're young and eager. We'll learn.

My daughter is very smart. She is the light of my life. She's what's kept me going through all of this. Her beautiful smile. Oh…and her ideas about England. She is so excited to be moving that she reads a lot of books about England. It's mainly about its history or Paddington bear but it's making her happy. She keeps telling me that she read in a book that children in England can do whatever they want and never get yelled at. Whenever I try to punish her for not listening or doing something naughty, she tells me, "That won't be allowed in London, Mama."

I don't think she quite understands how discipline works but I'm just excited that she's excited.

The Light of Our House
Karachi, Pakistan

Hiba's Story

I had a wonderful childhood. My father made sure of that. I was the youngest of four girls and most people would have been upset without a son but not my father. He named me Hiba which meant gift in Arabic. That's exactly what he saw me and each of my sisters as. Gifts from God. He has raised us all like boys. Independent and capable of whatever we set our minds to. He told all four of his daughters that they could do anything.

Once when I was young, I watched a rocket launch into space on our box TV. My father went the next day to the shop and brought me a model rocket. We made it together with my sisters and launched our rocket that night.

Many people in our community frowned upon how our father treated us but my father did not care. He didn't want his children dependent on anyone. If anything went wrong, he wanted us to know exactly what to do and be able to support ourselves. My father wanted us to have fun. We'd play cricket with the neighbourhood children. My father was always the umpire and my sisters, and I were always in (even when we were out). We'd ride on the back of his motorbike or fly kites on our roofs.

My father was the light of our house.

He had saved money for each of us to go to college. My eldest sister wanted to be a doctor from the moment she came out of the womb and my father had made sure she had every opportunity to achieve that. He was hoping though, that one of us would go into engineering – although none of us had shown any interest in it when we were younger. My father wanted to be an engineer and taught us all how to build things or fix motors. He never had the money to be an engineer himself, but he saved enough for one of us to be one. He wanted big things for us.

Whenever my mum asked us to help her in the kitchen, he would go in to help himself. He didn't want anything distracting us from our studies. Whether it was a small task or studying for our exams, education came first. I always appreciated this. Most of my friends would tell me how they would have to go home from school and help their mothers. Cooking dinner or cleaning the house before they could start their homework. I could never relate. My father came home from work and after a cup of tea, would be in the kitchen helping my mama. My sisters and I helped out when we could, but it was not expected.

He was killed in a suicide bombing in 2003, while he was attending Friday prayers. He always attended his Friday prayers. He always went to the same mosque. Along the same route. We were at home. We'd prepared a special lunch for him and were expecting him any minute. My sister had just passed her exams and was going to be a doctor. Suddenly our relatives began calling to ask if he'd been at the mosque and it was only when we turned the TV on whilst mama was on the phone, that we found out.

We rushed to the hospital to find him. It was chaos. We walked past many beds covered in white sheets. Many people lost their lives that day and there was this feeling. A small feeling in all of us that he had not made it. We showed his picture to anyone we could. Doctors, nurses and volunteers but no one had seen him. After hours of watching bodies come in and out of the hospital like luggage at the airport, an ambulance driver finally approached us when he saw my father's picture in my hand. The ambulance driver told us that he refused to be taken away and that he insisted they treat other people first. He was going to be one of the last bodies recovered from the wreckage. The driver thinks my father knew he would never make it. We believe he was martyred and those who are martyred never die.

My father left us a small, sweet message on our answering machine before he died. He said, "I love you all and follow what I taught you."

We think he's still with our family and shares our concerns. Whenever I am tense or nervous or achieve something big, I smell him. He had his own smell. I don't know how to describe it.

I'm now in my last year of university and training to be an engineer. Whenever I fix anything, I remember how happy I was when my father fixed my racing car. I hope I can give someone the same gift of happiness that he gave to me.

The Blood Man
Lagos, Nigeria

Kya's Story

I was born in Nigeria. I am one of five children that were born here. When I was little, my mother won the visa lottery. We packed up our entire life in Nigeria (which was about five bags for all of us) and relocated to Minnesota. My parents wanted us to have the best opportunity and they knew they couldn't provide that to us in Nigeria at the time.

I think I'm the only one of my siblings who always viewed Nigeria as home and Minnesota as just a pit stop on our way back.

In Minnesota, I got involved in all the subjects I took. I loved international political science. I participated in Model UN and always chose one of the countries from Africa. I admired Nelson Mandela and the message he stood for. I admired the positive change he wanted to bring. I always knew I'd go back to Africa one day; I just didn't know when.

After graduation, I interned with an NGO in Northern Nigeria. The trip was for a month and would let me see what it was like out there. I hadn't been to Nigeria in fourteen years, so I was very excited. During that trip, I helped out with many cases and realised quickly why my parents wanted us to leave. The resources were very limited, and the knowledge was only transferred so far. People were desperate for help, but the doctors could not reach everyone. The doctors I worked with prioritised people within minutes of meeting them. That was the hardest part for me. Some people were given death sentences by doctors after just two minutes of an assessment. I understood resources were limited and could not be wasted, but it was difficult to swallow. On some days I went into villages with the other NGOs. I witnessed a breached birth in a village. There was no C-Section available, so the baby died.

I knew then that not only would I be coming home to Nigeria, but I'd be doing something in healthcare. I wanted to help these people. My people.

I've been home in Nigeria for six years now. When I got back to Minnesota after my NGO trip, I looked into my different options and trained as a nurse. When I got home to Nigeria, I realised quickly that that was not what these people need and chose to work on the country's blood distribution problem. I'm still working with the same company I worked with six years ago.

Every year tens of thousands of people die while waiting for blood. While we have the supply most of the time, most places do not have a place to store the blood in the right conditions. Blood banks are scattered around Nigeria but often, those who need it most can't make the journey to get it. After a while, a lot of blood banks are discarding unused inventory.

My company is trying to close that gap between waste and demand.

Most blood banks in Lagos are participating in our program and it seems to be making a significant difference. Every morning we take an inventory and when blood is urgently needed, we use bikes to deliver. It's not an easy job. Being on our bikes is like being in the Centre of London without all the infrastructure, no underground train system and worn roads. However, we don't let that stop us. We've delivered over ten thousand bags of blood within fifty-five minutes when it's been needed.

Blood shortage is a global problem but if we all start in our own little places, we'll be able to start making a big difference. I think that if we can do it here, we can do it anywhere. We're hoping to expand to two new cities this year, but I see us all over the world.

That's what I'm working towards anyways.

Finding My Village
Manhattan, USA

Vivienne's Story

"It's so hard to ask for help."

You're expected your entire life to just know you're supposed to be 'Mummy'. That's what you were made to be. I didn't want to be the only woman to say, 'I need help being a mummy.' You never want to be the only person to say that. To feel that.

I carried this human for nine months. I knew she was coming.

That's what made me feel worse. I had all the books stacked up in my house about how to raise this child. My own mother made it sound like the most blissful and special moment of my life. I remember my mum telling me, "Vivienne, the hardest part – obviously after having to give birth, is probably going to be picking a name. It took me three months to choose yours and another two weeks after you were born because we just couldn't decide."

"Well, Mum, I flicked open the name book, landed on Julia and bam, that was my daughter's name. That was the easiest part of the whole process."

I think the biggest misconception that I had was that I assumed we'd instantly connect. I carried her for so long. She was literally a part of me. I assumed Julia would just know me and I would know her. That instant connection should have existed, but it didn't. Julia and I were two very different people, with two very different needs and we didn't understand each other one bit. I felt like I should have been able to handle it. I should have been able to begin to dissect through the vomit and the crying and the nappy bags to understand what Julia needed – or even in the ballpark region of what she needed. I didn't want to ask other people to stop their lives – especially if they had no part in making my baby.

There's a stigma attached to women. Working or staying at home. Women judge other women based on the choices they make and women in my baby and me classes were no different. Everyone there seemed to be living in bliss. Their children were sleeping through the night and easy during the day. Their partners were at work and would come home to spend time with their babies – when I say time, I think these women had their babies asleep by the time their partners walked in through the door. Their families were involved to help out on date nights – I couldn't believe they even had the energy or time for a date night. They were groomed models.

Having a baby was already difficult for me. Next to these women, it was even harder.

No one would talk about the constant crying at 2 am (then again at 4 am, 7 am and all through the day). No one spoke about the pressure of juggling this person with household work. I literally couldn't even use the toilet without hearing Julia cry. If I'm being honest, sometimes I just went to the toilet and let her cry, so I could cry by myself. I wouldn't say I had postpartum depression. I was just overwhelmed. I needed to do so many things, but my daughter didn't want me to do anything. Every time someone even tried to give me advice, I would feel like I was being attacked for my parenting.

I really thought I wanted a baby. Having her just made me question why.

Eventually, I had to give in. If I didn't, I would have had a breakdown. I'm just one person and being 'Mama' twenty-four/seven can make you crazy. There were times I just wanted to throw my child out of the window so she would stop. I still feel awful for feeling like that, but I was drowning.

I found myself getting frustrated that other people were going on with their lives. I'd let things fester and it was really unhealthy for my relationships. I'd get heated with my mother and my husband. Instead of beginning with 'can you help?' I'd instantly lose my temper, and jump straight to 'Why aren't you helping?'

We spoke for a long time – my husband Edward and I. My mother looked after my daughter whilst we did, and it was the most blissful few hours I had had in a long time. My mother also told me that it was not easy to raise me. She hadn't wanted to scare me whilst I was pregnant and covered up a lot of the more gruesome aspects of motherhood. She once forgot me in the house because I had made her so tired and hadn't realised until arrived at the grocery store half an hour later. She had never forgiven herself properly for that. She had never mentioned it before to me because I appeared to be coping so well. I didn't ever complain to people because I was a mother but being a mother doesn't come without its challenges.

The real adult conversation that night made me realise my family wasn't the family in almost every single help book. I needed to be realistic. Edward and I agreed that I would go back to work part-time, and he would take a few days off for a month to settle our baby girl into a routine. We realised that I needed to be both Vivienne and Mama but not necessarily at the same time.

I've had her for three years now and I haven't regretted a single decision since our conversation that night two and a half years ago. I learnt that it was okay for me to take a village to raise my baby. I didn't have to be an island all the time.

My relationship has never been better with my daughter or any other member of my family for that matter.

Musical Chairs
Phnom Penh, Cambodia

Botha's Story

The entertainment industry is like a game of musical chairs. Everyone playing wants to win but only luck and timing can choose a winner. That's what happened to me.

I was really lucky. I was in the right place, at the right time.

My mum and I had gone shopping in the market when a man noticed me. He spoke in great depth with my mum whilst she was picking vegetables for our dinner. The man said that I had all the qualities to be a model and that he was part of an agency that could help me pursue a successful career. He left us with his card, but my mum had already jumped at the chance. She wanted me to earn my own money and help support the family. Soon, my face was instantly recognisable as my life became more and more hectic with bookings. I was doing everything from catalogues to runways and soon enough, there wasn't a street without my face plastered on its poster.

It became apparent to me that my looks had now become my livelihood.

My birth name, Bopha, was no longer what I was called – it wasn't commercial enough. I simply went by Angela. My name spread across the industry and then a new opportunity came knocking on my door. Many producers wanted to use me as a music video girl. These were big jobs in our country and the money was nothing like I had earned before. After one job, another came and then another. They just kept rolling in. I became a music video star, featuring in over five hundred videos in just six months. There was one particular music label that hired me continuously – one of their producers was on set of one of the music videos and introduced me to their senior executive. Since then, it was really non-stop. I saw the sets and that music producer a lot.

I didn't realise it at the time, but it was extremely unhealthy for me and unsafe too.

The music producer and I became somewhat inseparable. He was extremely well connected and had a lot of influence over people in the industry. He found a way to be wherever I was. When you spend so much time together in a day, so often, it's inevitable that feelings would grow – and they did. What I didn't realise was how dangerous that could be. How toxic that is when you only have half a man to spend time with. When we were together, he wasn't all there. His attention was divided and he changed so quickly. He was in love with me, but his love was all-consuming. Possessive. When I needed him emotionally, he wouldn't be there for me, so I would sink my safety in other people and that would anger him.

As far as boyfriends go, he was insane. He often locked me in our hotel rooms. There was this one time I was locked in a room for ten days because he thought I would leave him. I found out he had a wife but by then it was too late. If I said no, my family would be in trouble. I could take a hit in my head or a punch in my stomach but my parents, they were fragile. They needed the money. Not the agony that this life also brought with it. I did whatever he asked but ultimately, everything came with a cost.

It happened when I was on my way to a video shoot. I was running late. He'd locked me up in his 'other' home for the weekend and I had to wait to be released by him. I was running in six-inch heels down the street because I didn't want to be seen as unprofessional. I was looking in my handbag for my entry pass when a woman with a clipboard came up to me. She pulled on my shirt, stopping me outside the building I needed to enter. She asked me my name and it felt like I was shouting it out – I was in such a desperate rush.

That's when my cost came.

Moving her clipboard, I saw a metal canister being propelled forward. Over my head came a caustic liquid that melted my skin. The flesh of my skin liquefied on its way down to my bone. I could hear this white noise as I cried out in pain. I threw what little water I had over my head, but it didn't help. I could feel my ear dripping off. I could see my vision blurring to darkness.

The process of recovery was long and traumatising. Every time I closed my eyes and I remembered it all. The sound of my sizzling flesh pierced my ears. The tingling sensation from the burns danced on my face. My heart thumped against my chest, just like it did then. Every time I tried to do anything, that's all I envisioned…all I felt.

Whilst in recovery, it was the first time I heard anyone call me Bopha again in seven years. I was fifteen when I last heard that name. My name. My own mother didn't even call me that anymore because Bopha didn't have an existence anymore. Angela. Angela. Angela. However, when I heard the nurse call me that, I remembered so much of my life. How simple it was when we were poor. We may not have had the same opportunities, but I had a father. I had a family. I could turn to my siblings for advice at any moment of the day. We laughed around the dinner table. Angela never got that. Her father passed away in a car accident on the way to her first photoshoot for a big company. Her mother was now a robotic manager. She now didn't even have time to eat food around the table. She shouldn't have even eaten. That's what really upset me.

The lights in my life seemed to have gone off for quite a while. I was blind in both my eyes. I had to have over twenty surgeries. I had two mental breakdowns, had to be kept on a Psych hold for two weeks after a suicide attempt and lost my career. My life was darkness. Both physically and mentally. It became harder when I learned that the woman who had done this to me would walk free. Her husband paid a lot of money to make the scandal go away. To make the judge look the other way when giving his ruling. He always said he could make anything go away as long as he paid the right people, the right amount. I didn't feel like I had anything left to fight for.

Running my hands over the wooden floor of my apartment one day, I felt the sun radiate on my face. My mum's voice quietly hummed in the background. She had come to visit me. I remember this one night, I was walking in my apartment, and I fell over this metal container. There was oil in it that had now spilt, and I had fallen into it. I thought if I could feel around and find a lighter, I could save myself. I could end my life and not have to worry anymore. About how I'd support my family. How I'd continue to pay for my surgeries. How I couldn't do anything because I couldn't even see. I found a box of matches next to the cooker – hearing the sticks bounce against the cardboard walls when I shook it. My mum ran in though and she held me so tightly around my waist that I just collapsed onto the floor in tears. It was like she was releasing a plug. I can't remember exactly how she did it, but she instilled this faith in me that night. She reminded me that I had used my looks up to this point, as it was a quick option but that I had a very powerful brain. That I could use it to do so much. I had already used it to pull through my extensive recovery process.

Working with my family, we now own a legal firm that has been operating for five years. I had paid for my younger brother to become a lawyer whilst I was modelling. He visited me during my physiotherapy sessions and revised for his exams whilst I did my exercises. I picked up a lot from his revision – my hearing being a lot sharper than it used to be. It made it a lot easier when I went to sit my bar examination. Angela doesn't exist anymore. She wasn't what I wanted or could be anymore. I live full time as Bopha. A strong, resilient, and intelligent woman. My family and I work on a lot of cases now, but I mainly focus on impunity. I try and get justice for as many women as I can so that those other attackers do not just get to walk away – like mine did.

Freedom to the Seventh Generation
Namakabroud, Iran

Mahdieha's Story

I grew up in a generation just after the Islamic revolution. It was very difficult for people to adjust. Especially those from smaller cities. As time passed, we had to conform because that was all we knew, but we are now starting to loosen ourselves.

Things are getting freer.

Even a few years ago, I couldn't wear what I'm wearing now without inviting a scolding. If I wore a scarf that was too bright, my sister Fatimah would say, "Mahdieha, Baba will tell you off for wearing that," or if I wore a pair of jeans she would say, "Mahdieha, you know mama will tell you to change out of that." A girl without a burka was not even a thought to most people. A girl like me today, in a three-quarter sleeve, knee-length top, was definitely not even a concept. Women have learnt to live more freely though. Our lipstick has got brighter, we've started acknowledging plastic surgery and our clothes are not always just black. We may not be screaming at the top of our lungs yet – we do not want to give our older generations heart attacks for the time being, but we have learned to loosen our limits. We were always our own boundaries.

The scarves are getting brighter and looser. The sleeves are getting shorter. The laughter is getting louder. Most importantly, our opinions are thoughts are getting heard.

Iran. This Iran. This Iran is a very young country. More than half the population is under thirty. Our ideas are changing and modernising with the times. We have embraced the opulence of our heritage and the strength of the revolutionaries. We are teaching our children the balance between the old Iran and the new. That religion and life can live in harmony. Have you ever seen an

Iranian child? Iranian children are the most mischievous, fun-loving and resilient children on the planet. If you want an Iranian child to do something, like most children – tell them not to do it. Tell them not to play out till late. Tell them not to eat sweets. Tell them not to dress in black. Tell them not to use Facebook.

This country is full of mischievous, curious Iranians. We're all looking to identify with our ideas and values. Our inner child is alive in all of us. With the help of our parents, we are learning that it's okay to follow broader ideas. Feminism does exist in our religion. Equality does exist in our religion. We just haven't been listening properly.

The people who make the rules are getting older. Just like the Iranian parent, they too are getting exhausted. Now is our time to be alive.

Independence – Not Isolation
Kabul, Afghanistan

Tamana's Story

I was raised watching my mother struggle. She didn't seem to exist outside of our house. She didn't seem to exist at all.

My baba or my bhai, Ahmed, would do everything for her. If she needed to go to the shop, they would go. If she needed to drop off some food for someone who was ill, they would go. If she needed to get a prescription, they would go. My mother only existed to make food or clean dishes or wash clothes inside the perimeters of our house. If a shirt needed to be ironed, Ahmed Bhai would always ask our mama. If Ahmed Bhai needed help with his maths homework, Ahmed Bhai would always ask our mama for help until Baba got home. He didn't appreciate how smart she actually was.

Whilst they were out at work or college, Mama helped me with all my homework. She taught me to read. She would help me with all my maths work. Even when she didn't know what to do, she would say, "Tamana give me your book for five minutes." She'd study it as quickly as she could and then teach me as if she'd known for years. Her favourite subject was Maths, and she was going to do a master's, but she ended up getting pregnant with my bhai.

My family saw my mama as just a housemaid. She woke up at six every morning to make food for everyone before they went to work, college, or school. She would go to sleep at midnight on most nights, after she had pressed everyone's clothes for the next day, had cleaned up and had eaten herself. If my mama ever tried to help or open her mouth with an opinion – which she did try to do on many occasions, she was instantly put down. My father said she didn't know what it was like out in the real world. She didn't know how difficult it was.

Mama swept all our issues under the carpet. She didn't want to create any more problems. A quiet life was all she wanted. She didn't like getting shouted at. She didn't like being a problem.

She always made an exception for me though.

It was always mama's wish for me to go to school and then college. She said it would get me better rishtas and this kept my baba quiet – as long as she paid for it herself. Mama had put aside a small amount of her household money every month for me. I didn't know until I got into college, but she had been saving for me since I was six. She even sold a gold set once when my baba went to Lahore for work one day. She said my education was more important than gold. I'm hoping to get her one just like the one she sold once I start working and have the money.

I want to have my own career. I learnt that from my mama. I don't want to depend on anyone else. I don't want anyone to put me down because they think I am less than them. My brain has no less space than a man. I can always learn the same as them. It's hard though. There's a view in our society that an independent woman doesn't belong here. She is not 'one of us'. Once you say you want to be independent, they expect you to do everything by yourself. They think you've somehow learnt five years' worth of knowledge overnight. That's the difficult part. People won't understand. They don't want to understand. Even Ahmed Bhai asked me, "Tamana, why are you making life harder for yourself? Do you want to grow up alone?"

Wanting to be independent doesn't mean I want to be alone. I just want to be able to make my mama know that her fight was worth it. That the brain she used to make me who I am today can one day change the world, all thanks to her.

Seeing the World Through Even Bigger Eyes
Sydney, Australia

Ruby's Story

We were so excited to be having another child. We weren't planning it – we already had one beautiful child, so this was just another blessing. We thought so much about what our child would look like. A boy or a girl. A little chubby or very skinny like its daddy. Big ears or a little funny looking. I don't think we minded as much what the baby looked like; we just wanted the baby to be healthy.

My pregnancy had been closely monitored from the beginning. I had had a very stressful first pregnancy and the second pregnancy being so close to the first raised some concerns for my doctors. The scans all said the baby was perfectly healthy. Ten fingers and ten toes were all we had really counted on when we went to our doctor's appointments. Oh, and a strong heartbeat of course – just in case the baby wanted to be an athlete.

It was one day during my last few scans that I remembered commenting – "My baby keeps looking like a little Buddha floating in the water." The sonographer raised an eye at me as she quietly called for a midwife. They refused to alarm me, but I could tell by how they were, that something was wrong. After a lot of long needles and tests, it wasn't until I gave birth, that we could see what the problem was. The doctors took my baby down to get checked and called in the specialist. They said, "Mr and Mrs Donovan, we're really sorry but we have to tell you that your baby has Down syndrome." It didn't feel like it was the end of the world to me. When they started speaking and I heard the word 'we're sorry', I thought we'd lost the baby, so hearing he was alive was all I cared about. It was a few hours later that it hit me.

Our baby had Down syndrome.

Initially, I was just grateful to have a breathing and otherwise healthy baby. The real stress was how I raised my child. Did I have to do things differently? Did I have to wrap him in cotton wool, or do I let him grow? Do I raise him like my son Evan, or do I need specialist help to care for him? Can I even care for him?

Once our baby Hart was in our arms though, I think all the worry washed from my face. I just knew he would show me what to do. However, I could tell most of my family and especially my husband was devastated. He thought the most he would be making fun of was our baby's big forehead. Not having to tolerate people making fun of him, his whole life. I could tell that if we had found out earlier, my husband would have probably told me to terminate my pregnancy.

Every day I look down at my baby boy Hart though, I'm glad I didn't. I'm glad I didn't know. I'm glad I wouldn't have had to face the pressure of any other option because, to me, my child is amazing.

I decided to take the bull by the horns in raising my two boys. It was definitely challenging though. I left work completely as my life became confused by my children. I gave my Hart a lot more attention than his older brother, Evan, but I didn't want anything to make Hart feel like he could be anything less. When he loved something or was passionate, I would provide him with an infinite amount of opportunities to do any activity relating to it. He went through a solar system phase, so I created an entire layout of the planets for his room with him – he even made one for Evan.

The relationship between my husband and me after his birth was a little tense. I think it was more because he was afraid that he wouldn't be able to look past his disability. My husband thought that every time he'd see Hart, he would only remember what he wasn't able to do. My husband had read a lot of things on the internet which made him very agitated but even though he didn't feel it in his brain, every time he held Hart his heart tugged. He felt a warmth from our little boy that he didn't with our first one.

We were all afraid when we first brought Hart home. We thought we would break him even more. We didn't think we could provide him with the love he needed. My husband took a long time to come around mentally but he never failed physically. After long days at the office, he would immediately come home and help me with the boys. He would let me spend some time with Evan whilst he soothed the younger one. My little boy was a blessing to our family. He made us all closer. We constantly spent every moment of the day thinking about how the other is doing. My elder son is still obsessed with asking me if I've given his little brother enough cuddles. He often tells me off because I don't do it properly – apparently, my four-year-old knows how to do the special hug for my one-year-old better than I do.

Evan loves being a big brother. He often comes home from school and tells me we have a better version than most people. I always laugh because in many cases it is very true. We have been blessed. Hart is carefree and ambitious. He knows no limits and we do not set him any. No mountain is too high for him. He expresses the emotions he feels. If he is happy, the whole house is bubbling with excitement. If he is sad, we can hear his cries from all four corners of Australia. If he's mad, our house is the colour red. My son never conceals his emotions but always expresses just how he feels.

There's no evil to him. Just a blissful innocence.

Don't Tell Me
Vilnius, Lithuania

Anna's Story

Do not tell me if you killed yourself, your best friends would not care. That they would not sit at your lunch table for three days staring blankly at your seat, wishing you were there to fill the air with laughter because we did. We wondered why you said you were fine every time we asked you if you were okay. When we saw you were sad, but you insisted that nothing was wrong and that we were worrying about nothing. That we should drop the subject. We wondered why you thought we weren't enough for you to confide in. Where we went wrong in letting you go home hours before you died because you told us that you just needed some space as you were just tired.

Do not tell me that even though you two never get along, your little brother wouldn't break down in the middle of class because they started talking about your favourite subject in school because he did. We volunteered to help his class that day and watched him drop to the floor in a flood of tears. Asking us what he did to push you so far away. If it was the last chocolate slice he ate in the middle of the night when he knew you wanted it. If it was because he slammed his room door in your face after you kept asking him to do his school homework, but he didn't want to.

Don't tell me your mother would not stare at herself in the mirror with trembling lips wishing she could be bringing you home from the hospital rather than escorting you out in a casket to the nearest cemetery because she did. We visited her every day after your burial and watch as she put on the last hoodie you wore, desperately trying to imprint your scent into her skin so she could remember every bit of you. Screaming at herself for missing all the signs even though she watched you every night. Eating your dinner, laughing whilst watching TV and having a warm cup of milk with her, whilst catching up on your days together.

Do not tell me your father would not begin working night shifts to distract himself from the silence at home because you're not up until an ungodly hour of the night talking to what's their face on the phone because you're in need of advice because he did. He was so scared to be in the house without you that he worked himself into the ground. We saw him every day at the supermarket. Whether it be to get the milk we ran out of on the way home from school or whether it be a late-night craving. He was there. He was clinging to the last post-it-note you had left him, tattooing your handwriting into his brain before every scrap of you would be taken from him.

Do not tell me your friends will not stare at the wooden wall in the hall after the headteacher announces your death to the entire school, making no sound and trying to convince themselves that this is just another one of your impractical jokes because we did. We waited for someone to wake us up and tell us that everything had just been an awful nightmare.

Do not tell me how the stars would still appear, and the sun will still come out. That the earth will still rotate, and the seasons will still change because without you no one would want any of those things to happen. You are important. You were worth it, but you didn't let us help you.

We've all spent hours of our lives wondering where we had gone wrong. What signs we missed. Why we didn't ask you just one more time if you were okay. Why we always accepted 'I'm fine' as a response to your feelings. Why didn't we insist on talking more about what was going on in your brain as opposed to what you watched last night on TV. We realised, we all asked you those questions, but you made yourself an island. That your illness had made you an island. You were so alone in your head that no one had any idea what was going on. On how far you would go.

Now, there's no you except for the you in our dreams at night.

Finding My Own Wings
Belgrade, Serbia

Odetta's Story

It was hard living back home. I come from a village that has very few resources. My parents were farmers and worked the land of our people. We used to have really good resources four generations ago, but the wars ruined the land and stole our animals. My dad had been working for years to rebuild his family legacy. He built up the animals and started to cultivate the land, but it wasn't enough.

For me, it wasn't anyway.

My little village is pleasant. The people are kind and mindful. We all look out for each other but there is no growth there. Financially. Mentally. It's very limiting. My country was beginning to feel limiting. The economy is not what it used to be. People are suffering and if I had stayed home, my life would have been nothing. I used to wake up in the morning, cook for my siblings, clean the house and repeat it again. Whenever I had any free time, I filled it with reading. We had a very basic library in our village, but the collection had grown over the years by students that had left our village and returned to visit family. There were some textbooks in there that I could barely understand but by learning the basics of English, all the books allowed me to escape and create so much more in my mind.

I wanted to do more with my life than what would have been possible in our village, so I'm currently working in the city so I can save for my education before moving abroad.

The experience hasn't been as liberating as I thought it would be. It's a lot lonelier. On the farm, my life revolved around my family's schedule. I'm now so much further from home than I expected. I don't have enough money to visit my family regularly – unless I don't want to save anything for university. I spend most of the evening alone in a single room at the boarding house I'm staying at.

I have nothing to do all day besides think of my family or distract myself with a book.

The city life hasn't been as wild as it's perceived. I've been here for a year but between working and being exhausted, I still haven't met that many people. Working is the only time I feel even the slightest spark of feeling. The feeling of home. My co-worker Dora is my closest friend – she's like my mother away from home. She's always looking after me; reminding me to take my medicines, eat and get enough hours of sleep. On the days she sees my heart breaking or sadness overtaking me, she tells me, "Odetta, take this one out," and does the rest of the work by herself – offering an ear to listen but expecting nothing more from me. The feeling of being cared for is so nice and something I'm still really missing.

I wouldn't say I'm homesick. I never miss the village, but I miss my family. I miss the hugs and even the telling offs. It's hard being out here alone but it has been worth it. Next month I will be starting my entry-level qualifications. I'll then be able to apply to university after that. I've done so much reading that I don't know what I'll quite study yet. The possibilities seem endless.

What I do know is, if I'm feeling stuck, I can ask my best friend Dora. Without her here, I don't think I could have made it.

The Theory of Life
Fes, Morocco

Daniya's Story

I like to sit alone and think about the world.

Ever since I was little. My mama got me a physics book with a small solar system. "Daniya, this should keep you busy for a while whilst I do some work," is what she said to me when she put it in my lap. It had pop out pictures. She was right, it did keep me occupied for days. It made me think.

How did everything begin? Are we really thinking logically? What else is there out there?

Since I was little, I learned to question everything. I knew there was always more than one perceptive and we need to examine all possibilities. Rationally. I always question myself. *Daniya, do you believe this to be true?* or *Daniya, do you think this could actually happen? If you really think logically about this, do you think it is possible?* My mum and dad always encouraged me to express my thoughts. Express my desire to need to know more. I believe that everything needed to be proven.

I wanted to be a philosophy major but there is no philosophy class at our universities. The only class offered is 'Religion and Philosophy' and that is quite different to what you would think. We aren't exactly encouraged to decide things for ourselves here. Any philosophy we have must be built on the existence of God, not science.

It was conflicting for a very long time. I wanted to learn so much more. I had so many more questions to ask but I couldn't live my life only building on God's existence. I do believe there is a God, but I cannot just believe that if God will's it, it will happen. I believe in logic. I believe in science.

I switched my major to physics last year. It still allows me to think about the world in the way that I want to but now if someone wants me to say that a thing is true, they need to prove it with a formula. Not with a religious quote.

A House Full of Hope
Cairo, Egypt

Saleema's Story

My father was very strict with us.

I think it was the way that he showed his love, but it meant my sister Tayana and I were often trapped within the confines of our home. Mama left the house sometimes but even then, she tried not to. She didn't like the comments he made afterwards. His workshop was right across the street from our building, and he'd scream if he saw us peeking out the window. Life at home felt like it was a prison.

We'd just stay at home. My mother would sometimes encourage us to read but she didn't put too much emphasis on it. "Saleema what do you need it for? Look at me, I have a degree and all I do is stay in the house all day." We mainly spent our time making Father tea, food and watching TV.

Back then it was mostly black and white movies starring Egyptian icons. The movies were like an escape for me. They gave me an idea of what life was like outside. In the real world. I'd dream about that often. My favourite movies were love stories, but they were just fantasy. My father rejected all my suitors.

During that time, my only escape from my home was my grandmother's house. She was everything to me. She knew what her son, my father, was like so she exposed me to glimpses of the real world. She took me shopping, out to lunch and to her group gatherings. She wanted me to be able to stand on my own feet as there were no guarantees in life. That's why she wanted my mother to marry her son. My grandmother had been widowed at a very young age and raising her two sons had been very difficult. She thought an educated woman would help to ensure that her grandchildren would be well educated – to break a cycle of sorts, but nothing came of it. My mother had crumbled under the demands of my father.

I fell in love with my grandmother's neighbour. He was tall, light-skinned, and wore his hair combed back. He often ran over to help with the shopping when we'd come back. He had this aura about him that never quite went away. I'd visit her on many occasions just so I could see him. My grandmother quickly knew. She noticed how much I'd smile after he came around. She'd started to tell my father she wanted me to come around wearing my loveliest dresses so she could show me off to her friends. At first, he refused but she wore him down quickly. My grandmother would fix my hair and invite him over for tea and baklava. He'd always smile at me.

I was pretty back then. I loved him and he loved me. He told my grandmother that he wanted to marry me. I really wanted to marry him too.

My father arranged my marriage to my cousin though. My grandmother tried really hard to break it off. She even threatened him, "Aroob, if Saleema is forced to marry him, I will not speak another word to you. This is not a right match for Saleema." It didn't matter what she said though as my father was too stubborn to give up and she passed away shortly after my engagement. My mum saw how upset I was but there wasn't anything she could do.

My father married me to my cousin and that's when the real tragedy began.

I gave birth to one child after another. I did not want to have kids. I wanted to start my education but the promises before marriage and life after were very different. My husband was very lazy. He had a job when we first got married but left it over a pay conflict. He didn't think to find another job. As time went on, the bills kept coming and the money just kept finishing. I felt ashamed to ask my father for money, but I kept having to go home and ask. He saw it as my fault for not keeping my husband focused. How was I meant to focus on someone who just wanted to spend the day drinking it away?

I've had to work full time because my husband was so useless.

I live next door to my first love now. I moved into my grandmother's house after I walked out on my husband. My children were old enough to understand we were better off without him. My father had given me the house as a wedding gift because he knew how important it was to me. I never lived in it with my husband. I didn't want him to taint it for me. This house held all my happiest memories.

I see my first love often through my kitchen window. He has a university degree and every time he sees me, he smiles. He got married a few months after me, but his wife passed away last year from breast cancer.

My divorce is finalising, but I don't want to remarry yet. I want to stand on my own feet. I want my children to see that they don't need to be taken care of by someone else. My girls are given the freedom to live the life they want. I have told them my expectations and that some people will make comments. They know they are a reflection of me. My boys are given the same freedom as my girls. I'm teaching them to be respectful of women – to not treat them like prisoners or objects.

I'm raising my kids with tolerance and freedom. I'm working a good job and providing a halal life to my child.

One day I hope I'll be ready to move on but for now I'm happy finding Saleema. A Saleema that is free of all chains and full of possibilities.

Falling Under the Pressure
Riffa, Bahrain

Razia's Story

My mum has always been ill.

Since I was little, I remember my father having to get a carer for her. We had someone to help with the cooking and cleaning and another lady to look after my sister and me until my father came home. My mum still tried to be actively involved in our lives. She couldn't move a lot, but we sat with her. She read us stories and changed the characters' names, so they were ours – Sara and Razia fighting crime as a superhero dream team. She helped us with our homework. She fed us soup when we were ill – sleeping us next to her so she could be there if there was a problem. She tried her best, but her health kept deteriorating and only got worse when my father passed away.

My mum had nobody to care for her but me. My sister got married and moved to another city with her husband. My husband passed away a couple of years after we got married. He was in the Bahraini army so let me stay with my mum whenever he was deployed so that she had someone to look after her and so that I was not alone when he was away. Unfortunately, he was involved in a helicopter crash during one of his deployments and he passed away. That was a hard day in my life, but I had to fight on. I had my mother to take care of and a small child.

My mum's health had taken a turn for the worse in recent years. The last stroke affected her brain so badly that she was like the living dead. All she could do now was breathe. It pained me to see her like that, but I knew there was nothing I could do but pay for a doctor to help her and pray to God to save her. A few months ago, I found a tiny wound on her toe and thought it was just something small. It looked so small that I just put a bandage on it, but I made a mistake. It was the beginning of gangrene. I should have known. It spread so quickly that the doctors had no option but to amputate her leg.

It was all my fault, but I was under so much pressure.

I'm a single mother. I worked as a housekeeper. My life is not as luxurious as my childhood. I don't earn a lot of money and got no additional support. I had to look after my mum, my child and run a house. I had to stretch both myself and my money. What do I focus on? What do I pay for? My child's education? Food? My mum's care? It just got to be too much.

It was all on me.

I called my sister one week and just screamed at her. I screamed at her for never calling. I screamed at her for not helping. I was under so much pressure and my network of support had deteriorated. I had no one to help me. No one to even vent my feelings to. I told my sister that I wished my mother would die.

My wish came true. Four days later she passed away damaged and broken. I felt so awful. I was ashamed of how I behaved. How I thought. I was more upset because I now had to answer to my father, and he would be so upset about the state I had let my mother decline to. I'm sure he'd have been forgiving because I did try my best…but I felt like that still wasn't good enough.

When I saw my mother at the morgue a few days later, she had no hair, no eyebrows, nothing. The doctor told me she had fought a valiant war but ultimately the cancer had won. I remember standing frozen when the word came out of her mouth. Cancer. She had been hiding cancer from us – from me.

I still feel so guilty. My wish came true. I didn't eat properly for a few days afterwards. Only a cup of milk. Everything felt like it was crushing me. Even just waking up in the morning, I felt like a failure. Like I was doing it wrong. It got to be too much pressure.

I sent my kids to my in-laws' house for a few weeks and after non-stop housekeeping jobs, I finally got around to cleaning my house. I had left my mum's room just like it was on the day she died. I threw out a lot of rubbish. It had been piling up for years as she never let me throw her things out. Even when she became completely immobile. I found an envelope addressed to me in the mess. I hadn't seen it before, but it was probably because it was buried under so much mess. I remember sitting on her bed to read it. It was dated not too long before my mother had died. She told me, "My Habibi Razia, you've been too hard on yourself. You have always been the light in my life that has never gone off. Even when I thought it was going to begin to flicker."

That letter changed the way I thought about myself. I keep it in my purse for the days I need an extra boost. My third year of nurse training has been hard, but her letter keeps me going.

My mother named me Razia meaning content or satisfied. I finally feel that now.

Learning to Daydream
Lae, Papua New Guinea

Ana's Story

When I was younger, I hated reading.

My mother always told me books would be my greatest solace but at the time it felt like the biggest pain. I tried to avoid them as much as I could. My father only had religious books in the house for a very long time. The books felt familiar to me – I was actively practising the life they wrote about, so why did I have to read them?

It was only when I started studying that I realised the magic my mother spoke of. I was welcomed into a life so unfamiliar and so vulnerable, yet so enjoyable. I read so many different literary works. Shakespeare to Rumi. Every time I finished one, I felt privileged to have been able to go on that journey with the protagonist. To have lived a more travelled life and bring some of each character into me.

I've fallen in love with literature.

I try to read for one to two hours every day, but I often lose time falling into the rabbit hole that is these novels. I think the biggest thing these books have taught me about life is that you can't just skip chapters. You have to read every line and meet every character. You won't enjoy all of it otherwise. Some chapters make you want to cry for weeks. You will read things you don't want to read. You will have moments when you don't want the pages to end, but you have to keep going. Stories keep the world revolving and you don't want to miss out because you're looking to be just a chapter in someone else's.

I only have one life to live but with books, I can live a thousand.

They Don't Know Where I Go
Peshawar, Pakistan

Nadia's Story

We're present at births and weddings, having our own particular manner of dance and entertaining the masses. We put smiles on our faces but inside we feel like caged monkeys.

I was born in a brothel. The first boy to come into such a large group of women for over ten years. For most people that would have been great news but in a brothel, life and worries are very different. These women feared what would happen now. I was not worth anything of monetary value to them – I could not continue their cycle as a girl could. As a boy, they also worried about what would happen when hormones kicked in. Would I start assaulting the women in my own home? The women consulted a doctor and decided to prevent the problem before it became one. I had my private parts removed before the age of one.

Growing up I always identified myself as a woman. I had grown up wearing women's clothing – bright colours of plum red and golden yellow, makeup and involving myself in every way a woman would in society. I never once felt like a man because those feelings had been suppressed from such a young age. I was raised as a woman. In my heart and my head, I am a woman.

Society is still not so understanding. We are perceived as a third gender, and we have been acknowledged by the law. However, wherever we go, we are harassed, we are taunted, and we are expected to be entertainment. We are recognised as a third gender, but we are treated as third-class citizens.

Being transgender, we are expected to go everywhere and dance or beg for money. People expect transgender people to be in the prostitution business. I had left my family at the brothel when they too expected me to sell myself in this way. I did not want that life. I had seen how those women were treated and I wanted to be different. There wasn't much for me when I left the brothel. I did have to dance or beg because I had no other options. I refused to go any further though. However, when we are out on the streets and begging for money so we can feed ourselves and we refuse to be prostitutes because most of us are not, we get shot, beaten or humiliated for saying no. This is exactly what happened to me, but my nightmare did not end there.

I was shot on a very public street after a group of my friends, and I were on the way back from a party we had been invited to. People kept pulling down their windows as we walked up to our house and shouting rude remarks, but we ignored them. One man grabbed me by the arm and propositioned me. He asked if I would dance for him. I said no. He then started to push me against the wall as my friends shouted for help. He asked if there was somewhere we could take it further because he understood what I meant. I said no. He asked again and my reply was the same. No. He pulled out his gun from his jacket pocket and shot it at my stomach then my arm and then my leg. Laughing as he got on the back of his motorbike.

My friends rushed me to the hospital. When I got to the hospital, my blood was gushing out and I was losing consciousness. The doctors spent a lot of time deciding where to place me. I told them I was a woman but when I was moved towards the women's side there was a protest. They then transferred me to the men's side of the hospital where there was also a protest. The doctors cared more about where to place me than on where to start with the multiple gun-shot wounds I had. I was not seen as a victim but more as an issue. One transphobic doctor was so curious if my friend had real breasts or stuffed oranges in their top that he stopped moving my bed and asked them; refusing to believe either of their answers. When a call came in on his phone, he stopped pulling my bed and ran off with the nurses somewhere else. I was left unattended for an hour, and I had to wait for a further five before I was seen again. I'm fortunate that my friends have come across experiences like this before. They applied pressure to all my wounds and did their best to keep my blood circulating – using their own clothes to increase the pressure around my wounds.

In the time we were forced to wait, my friends were taunted and harassed by health technicians. My head may have been light and my eyesight blurred but my hearing was able and my heart broke as I heard them. As my friends begged for someone to save my life, they were being integrated about their 'nightly rate' and whether their services were limited to dancing alone or sex on-demand as well. Every time they asked a doctor to help, the nurses and technicians mocked that they would have to perform first. When police arrived at the hospital to enquire about my wound, they threatened to arrest my friends if they came too close to them – the police officers taunted them by saying that they did not want to catch anything from them. As soon as the police found out I was transgender, my case was no longer important. They packed up and left without even asking what happened.

Eventually, I was treated outside the toilet. By the time I received my treatment, I was unconscious and don't remember anything but what my friends told me. They removed the bullets from my body and had to transfuse blood – ten bags worth. When I came back around, an elderly doctor was standing in front of me reading my chart. I was now in a private room and my friends were all asleep on the sofa in front of me. I looked at the man, scared at what my friends had to do to get me my treatment. I was worried I had become too much of a burden on them now as well. The gentleman recognised the panic on my face and reassured me that the expense of my room and hospital treatment was on him. One of my friends had done him a favour but not like I thought.

A year ago, a friend of mine was called to his home for his son's wedding. Whilst they were there, the doctor's daughter got talking with my friend and told her that she had been married for four years and had not been able to conceive a child yet. My friend told her that there wasn't as much magic in her as people believed but she would make a special prayer for her. A few weeks later she found out that she was pregnant and nine months later she had a healthy, baby boy. The doctor had longed for a grandchild and that boy brought him more joy than anything he could have imagined. He remembered the face of my friend before their group left his son's wedding. As she walked out the door, his daughter pointed her out and told him how she had never met anyone kinder or more magical. He always wanted to repay the debt and now he could.

I've been recovering from my injuries for six months now. It's been difficult as it's prevented me from earning any money. I do not have the strength to dance or beg.

Society here recognises us as a third gender, but we still have a long way to go before they start recognising us as anything other than third-class citizens.

Making Sense of It
Accra, Ghana

Lulu's Story

I had some experience with abuse as a young child. It was always uncomfortable because the man that did it was a family friend.

Every time he came around our house, my dad would always tell me to cover myself up a bit more. It was like my dad knew he was a monster but thought because they were good friends, he wouldn't do anything to his daughter. He was so wrong. The first few times he visited; I never hid in my room. My dad didn't expect me to. I wasn't the man's best friend, but I would sit in my living room playing with my dolls or have a tea party with my teddy bear friends in the kitchen. I didn't do anything to lead him on. I've thought about it a lot. I kept thinking maybe it was my fault, but it wasn't.

After the first 'incident' I locked myself in my bedroom for three days. I told my parents I was just feeling sick and didn't want to be bothered. I was bleeding so heavily during those days I thought I was going to die. I wanted to die. He came around again a few days later after hearing I had been unwell. He brought me a teddy bear. He did it again that night.

Every time my dad asked me to make him a cup of tea, I wanted to vomit. Every time I heard him knock on the door, I wanted to throw myself out of my window. I couldn't even kill myself, I thought, though. If anyone found out about what had been happening after I died, people would assume I was promiscuous. That I wanted to do it.

Victims are shamed in our culture, so I couldn't talk to anyone. That's the problem with our society. We still teach our girls shame. Close your legs, and cover yourself. We make them feel as though being born a female should already make them feel guilty about something. Girls grow up to be women who can't say they have desires. They silence themselves. They grow to be women who cannot say what they truly think. I've seen some of the strongest women I know, crumble next to men because they've been taught to be inferior. I think the worst thing we have been taught is that we have to grow up to be women who have turned pretence into an art form.

I had to deal with it myself. I had to grow out of it.

The abuse continued for three years. The first year was a real struggle for me. I tried to cope by reading books about the human brain, learning how to compartmentalise when he touched me. I wanted to be able to forget that those moments even existed. I prayed to God every night for three years to end my misery. One night whilst I was praying, my dad ran into my room to break the news to me. His friend had been killed in a gunfight. I dropped to my knees, and I thanked God all night because my prayers had finally been answered.

That was not the end of it though.

The scars he left on my brain were deep. I learned how to heal and move on, and not be bitter but I still wore a mark of shame in everything I did. I made myself smaller in every situation. If a man walked in, I sat as far from him as possible. If anyone touched me, even my mother, I would freeze and just panic.

It was much later that I discovered that everything I wanted to learn and know was something called 'psychology'. I looked into it and enrolled in a class at my local community centre. It was a small class and only ran twice a week, but it helped. I only wanted to get to the point where I didn't feel ashamed anymore. The more I learned, the more I became determined to feel comfortable with sex. I didn't want this one man to ruin my entire future. I wanted to be my old self again and I just had to find her.

I joined all sorts of online forums. Women who were abused. Men who were abusers. Child abuse. Long term. Short term. Men. Female. Anything and everything I could. I learned so much that I decided to become a mentor of some sort. I decided that the stigma to end shame started with one person and there was no reason that that person could not be me. I became an educator. I've moderated about fifteen discussions so far. I wanted people to feel comfortable talking about the aftereffects of abuse. People don't think about that part – it's just presumed you've moved on but it's a long-term battle. I want people to ask me about how they carry on. How do they have a normal relationship? How do they try to have any form of intimacy when all they remember is those awful moments? I've spoken at church groups. I've spoken at schools. I think it's important to educate those younger than me on the topic – not just to stop there being a stigma but to prevent the problem before it even happens.

Along my journey, I've met a lot of women who share my experience. Family. Relatives. Close friends. Strangers. It makes no difference how you know them or who they are because the psychological effect is the same. I've started a small anonymous ladies' group that I run once a week. It's not well known among all the people in my community, but it is well known amongst the women. It was actually their idea. Some elderly women that I grew up knowing, attend the group. They too share my story, but they hid it so well.

It's taken a lot of courage.

We still have a long way to go. People in this country are still not very understanding. They think that if you're speaking about it, you're encouraging it, but I think it's the taboo of the matter that's harmful. Why not explain sex to kids? We tell them how to do everything else. They need to know that these feelings are natural but that they have a brain to keep them in check. They need to know that just like everything else has a right and wrong, there is a right-wrong in this. Consent is so important. Either we educate people about sex, or they'll be confused by it and if they're confused by it, they'll be shamed by it. If they're shamed by it, they'll be controlled by it.

Throughout this whole process, I kept wanting to be my old self again, but I realised, I was now nothing like her. I was stronger, braver and a lot less guilty. I didn't wear a scarlet letter anymore. I didn't wear a mark of shame because I had nothing to be ashamed about.

It was through education that I can now look back on my own experience. I realised how wrong it was for my father to even suggest to a nine-year-old girl to cover herself up when she was wearing a t-shirt and a pair of jeans in her own home. My father should have known that if he had to protect his daughter's image around someone who might have been triggered by the skin on a child's arm, then he shouldn't have been around someone like that. I learned that the blame society would have given me if I spoke up was misplaced. They might not have been educated on the matter, but I did nothing wrong. I have nothing to be ashamed of.

This can't control me anymore.

A Dash of Hope
Rome, Italy

Marina's Story

My husband and I have always been in a partnership. If he has an off day, I pull him back in. I make it better. If I have a bad day, he makes me smile. He makes it better. When we first got married, we made every decision together – even if it was minor. As time went on and we got busier raising three boys whilst working, we began to make them on our own, but we knew what the other one thought. We were in sync with one another, so it didn't matter. We could decide for both of us.

My husband is a mechanic. He learnt about cars when he was little – around the age of ten. He would work on them with his father or his uncle. As time went by, his passion for them grew so he got a job at a local shop at the age of fifteen whilst still going to school. My husband saved his money and eventually – with a bit of help from his father, brought a small workshop. He's been working as a mechanic there ever since. He works tremendously hard, but his business is slow.

It's not enough for our family.

When I see my children happy, I feel happy. Every time I pay their school fees, they tell me, "Mama you are the best mama." I feel bad when there are opportunities that they cannot do because we cannot afford them. I feel like I'm failing them when I have to say no to their big opportunities. My husband and I are even struggling to pay for their schooling, so we decided together that I would also start working. I'm selling newspapers and sweets so my children can go to school. I want them to be better than me. I want them to be someone great in this country. Someone who does not have to struggle and is respected by their community. If I have to be out here all day in the sun all day so that dream can happen, so be it.

My work does not stop on the streets outside my home though. I go home, I cook, I put them to bed, I do some housework and then I go to sleep. It's difficult because I want to do more but my time is already very stretched.

This past week has been my most difficult. I've been sick with malaria. We've had to take me to the hospital – although I did plead against it, and that cost us a lot of money. It was even worse because I haven't been able to work this week so I did not have extra money to cover the cost of my treatment. My husband wants me to rest and not be stressed. He thinks it's making it worse, but my children are beginning to cry from hunger and are desperately calling for me when they come home from school. My husband is trying to cope with everything – the finances, the children, the housework, his workshop, but the stress is too much for him alone.

I heard them all crying outside my bedroom the other day in the early hours of the morning. I remember lying in bed and just continuously praying, "God, help me go sell." It didn't help though. I tried so many times to get up and go outside, but every time I went my fever was too high, and I felt my body giving way. I was cold. I was dizzy. I had to go back inside.

I went back to work yesterday but my day did not go well. I woke up feeling great. I had no headache, my body was not cold, and I had a lot of energy. By ten o'clock it got really bad. My headache was vicious, my body was freezing and there was pain all over. I made enough to pay for the week's supply, but I've decided this is not enough.

I'm going to go back to school part-time so I can complete the next level of my English qualification. I want a better job so that I don't have to worry about my children if I'm ill or something worse happens to me. My husband works and he works very hard but that is not enough. I need to make sure my children are protected in case anything happens.

I want them to be okay.

The Music and Me
Hunza Valley, Pakistan

Saira's Story

I have always talked at the top of my lungs. Ever since I was a little girl. If I heard a noise, my voice would change to that tune.

When I was younger, my baba would get a new Bollywood videotape every Sunday from our corner shop. It wasn't the best copy, but it was enough. I watched all the musical numbers with doe eyes. The dancing. The singing. The performance. I used to watch the same movie every single day that week. I learnt all the songs and all the dance moves. I performed them for my baba and mama on Saturdays before we got our new film. I did this until I turned eleven and Baba got me a guitar. I then started teaching myself between homework and would play by ear whatever I heard on the TV.

I wanted to be a singer. I loved music. I practised all the time and worked on writing songs for myself. I especially loved sad songs – the words were always more poetic and related more to so many people.

My father always supported my dream. He wanted me to be happy. But the community put a lot of pressure on my mother. My father passed away when I was twelve. And everyone kept telling my mother that a girl could not be something like a singer without her father's permission. My father wouldn't have minded, but my mum was so worried about what people would think. She knew how cruel people in our community could be. Once one person knew, everyone knew. No one missed their chance to make a comment. She begged me to stop. She started to become very nervous every time I picked up my guitar. She didn't want me to stop. She knew it would make my father happy that I was still doing something I loved but she wanted to protect me the best way – the only way, she knew how.

I came home one day and placed 4000 Rupees on the table. My mum was confused as to where the money came from. I finally told her, "It's okay, Mum. I've sold my guitar. I'll stop."

Now I still want to be a professional musician, but I get great pleasure from teaching the next generation. I joined our local school and have started teaching the children how to play the guitar – I even made enough money to buy back the guitar my father had brought me. People still make comments but now the issue is with me working. My mum has learnt to ignore all the extra noise and I'm proud of her for standing on her own two feet – just like she is proud of me for still doing something that I love. There's just the two of us but we both earn enough to live comfortably and most importantly, we're both happy.

It's too sad for me to sing anymore but I never miss a note on my guitar. When I play it, I always feel like my father's looking over my shoulder.

Heartbreak on a Starry Night
Madrid, Spain

Josie's Story

I've spent most of my childhood and teens rebelling against my parents. I grew up in a very strict society. My parents tried to loosen the reins at home, but I always felt the need to break them. I wanted to feel free.

When I was sixteen, my parents let me go out with my friends to a cinema. I saw a boy when we were leaving. I don't remember anything about that film that day. I just remember him.

Over the next few months, I snuck around with him. He was so charismatic. So different to anything I'd experienced before. He let me have my own opinions and let them be different to those of the law. He never made me feel like I needed to be reined in. I was free when I was with him. I could be whatever I wanted. An artist. A scientist. A poet. He became everything I thought about. Day or night. He was like coming up for fresh air.

When I was eighteen, I told my parents I had found my soul mate and I wanted to marry him. I told them I was sure; I'd known him for two years now. I was certain I'd known everything about him. His favourite food. His bedtime rituals. The present his family got him for his seventh birthday. I was certain that I'd found the one. My mum and dad did not trust him. They didn't know him and they couldn't bring themselves to respect someone who spent time with their daughter in the darkness like thieves in the night.

On one occasion, I saw text messages from other women on his phone. This was whilst I was trying to get my parents on side. I was reassured that this was just because we weren't married. Mistakes that would not happen again. I blindly believed him. All I could see was him in shades of gold. My parents warned me about him and told me that if I went ahead with this, I would have to spend the rest of my life without them.

I married him anyway, without their permission.

My life has been ruined ever since I made that decision. I had no honeymoon phase. I had nowhere to go back to. I destroyed myself.

I thought he'd change. He kept telling me it was a one-off and I believed him because I thought I could go back to my teenage days with him. Sitting on a small brick wall just outside of our town during sunset. Sharing our dreams and ambitions. We were on one road. Now he leaves for days at a time. He's changed his tune. He tells, "You're overreacting. It's nothing. They come and go. But I'm here with you. I live with you."

I can't. My mind wanders with thoughts. I left my family for the road of roses I was promised. I can't calm down. Not when all I see is my father's eyes well with tears as he let me leave. I think about it all the time. I think about all the messages I've come across on his phone. Whenever he's out, I think about it. I try to stay busy and calm my mind, but it's gotten so bad that I'm seeing a doctor.

Recently, I left him. It all got too much for my health. I moved away from the city and have set up refugee with a women's group. I'm trying to help other women who have also been fooled like me and who have lost things. It's a slow process but I think it's helping me become more of the person I was before I met him.

I want to call my parents and tell them they were right. I want them to know how truly sorry I am. I just can't bring myself to tell them. I'm scared that once I start talking, I won't be able to stop.

Right now isn't the time for me but I hope I'm ready to call them soon. I think I really need them. I haven't felt like I've been my true self since I left them.

Yahoo
Lagos, Nigeria

Messina's Story

Lagos is flooded with gang culture. They're recruiting more and more young people who see it as a desirable career. They call themselves Yahoo Boys after the days when they used to use Yahoo email accounts to scam people.

I've heard of them around town for a while, but it was only when I went to the University of Lagos that I saw them. They form these little gangs and travel around in convoys where all the cars are the same colour. They line the street in their cars and make sure their presence is known.

They're not even like normal gangs anymore. They're like licenced businesses. They're always on their laptops, talking about their targets as clients and starting charity organisations. They rent office space and invest the money they get from their fraud business into other businesses.

Their true colours are shown on their Instagram accounts. Some of them have hundreds of thousands of followers. They brag about their life on there by posting pictures of their clothes and their cars. No one ever mentions where the money has come from, but everyone knows.

I sell art on the side whilst studying law. The gang have brought a lot of property around my university and where I sell my artwork. A lot of them buy art from me. Their fraud is predominantly based on emotion. They've asked me a lot for advice on things that women would say in a relationship. Sometimes they'll ask me to pick up their phone and pretend to be a secretary. I never participate because I know what it's like to be struggling. The boys have started to become a bit more aggressive recently and tried to bribe me into helping them through my paintings. I've just stopped selling my paintings to them. It's cost me a lot, but I can't take their money without feeling obliged to help them in return.

The gang left me alone for a few months. They didn't approach my art stall or hover around me in the streets around the university. That was until May. I was driving my friend's car to university because my car had broken down when suddenly I got boxed in by a group of cars and was forced to pull over. I turned off the engine when a boy with a gun stood right in front of my car but only pulled my window down slightly as another approached me from the side. I knew how these boys worked and didn't want to get stuck.

The boys began to harass me. They had a police officer with them who demanded I get out of my car. When I refused, they started calling me a prostitute. I told them I'm an artist and that I was running late – that people were expecting me. They did not care and started investigating the content inside my vehicle. They saw my laptop in the backseat, and they tried calling me an Internet scammer. The police officer said that he had seen me speaking with the boys on numerous occasions and that he could have me imprisoned for years if I did not cooperate. They asked me to open my computer and type in the password. I told them I couldn't do that, so instead they asked for a huge bribe. I repeated that this would not be possible, and I could not do that.

That's when it escalated.

Every single one of them cocked their guns at me. One of them got in the front seat and another got into the back seat. They both pointed their guns at me and told me to drive to an ATM. Feeling the cold metal against my neck, they both followed me out of the car towards the ATM. I left the car running. I maxed out one of my cards and told him that I have to go back and get another one. I walked slowly towards my car as one of them started trailing behind me. I jumped into my car, locked the doors and started driving away. That's when they started shooting at me!

All of this was captured on surveillance cameras.

I sped away. It felt like a film, but this was the reality of where I lived. I was taking shortcuts and back roads. I took as many turns as I could just to make sure they didn't catch me. The whole time I was thinking I'm about to get killed. When I got home, I found four dents in the car from where the bullets hit. I ran into my house and cried my eyes out all night. I hid under my window ledge just in case they found me. They had connections. Big connections, so I didn't want to take any chances.

A couple of days later, I contacted the police, but they wouldn't even speak to me unless I deleted the story from social media. I said, "I'm not doing that. I'm a law student."

I still haven't got justice for what happened to me but I'm working towards changing things. I still go to the same university – I didn't want them to think they could scare me. I've started a group to help raise awareness of the growing gang problem here in Lagos. I wanted to create a safer space for young people to come to instead of them being targeted by the Yahoo boys. Girls are being given additional self-defence classes too as their targets are predominantly female. They're a start to the problem until I can do better. I'm going to use my degree to make a change because I know I'm not the only one. Not everyone else would have been as lucky as me to escape either.

The Struggle
Port-Au-Prince, Haiti

Bianca's Story

I want to live a happy life.

I'm tired of having a poor life. I'm trying to save money for school, but nothing is working. That's the problem in countries like mine. There's a tax for being poor. The poverty tax. It doesn't involve the government taking away a little bit more of your money. It is far greater than money. It's the loss of life. Of experience. Of opportunities. The poverty tax for me means that my dad has been begging me to get married since the age of ten because he has struggled to afford me. At least it's not been as bad as my best friend. She was sold when she was ten and I haven't heard from her since. There is no opportunity to educate yourself further when you are poor because you just can't afford to do so. You have to give up something just to survive.

My desire for education outweighed anything else. My father told me to be a realist, so I left home to make it happen.

I've worked three jobs since leaving.

The first time I found a job, it was as a housekeeper. It was in the city, and they paid extremely well. It was a family of four and I felt really confident that I would be able to start university by the end of the year. I enjoyed it for the first month but then things started to change. Masks came off. Every morning I got dressed in my room and the man would try to touch me. I'd lock my door before I went to bed, but he had a spare key and wasn't afraid to use it. I was only seventeen. He wouldn't even stop when I threatened to tell on him. I even threatened to expose him to his wife and children but he knew how to spin the story and when I eventually told his wife what he was doing, his wife blamed me for his attention. She said I walked around asking for it with the way I dressed. I wore the uniform she gave me on my first day, every day when I worked. She beat me severely as he watched. The bruises were all over my body. There were times she wouldn't even allow me to eat because her husband looked at me in a certain way and that was my fault. I tried to stay because I wanted to go to school so badly.

Then one morning when I knew the whole family had gone to work or school, I went to take a shower. The house was empty, but I still locked the door out of habit. It wasn't long before the man was back in the house and trying to rape me in the bath. That's when I finally ran away and had to go back home until I could find something else.

My father's constant comments about giving up drove me to find another job quickly and within the week I found a new housekeeping job. I checked out the house before I applied because I didn't want to have to suffer again. I needed my education. It was an elderly couple with no children. The wife was a housemaker and the husband a pastor. I started working on a Monday but had to leave by that Friday. The same thing happened to me again. He kept trying to touch me inappropriately and when I really shouted at him, he pushed me against the wall. I kicked him in the stomach and ran.

A few weeks ago, I switched to a cleaning job at an art gallery. It was less money but safer. I was constantly in a public space. People were watching me. I was working in the daylight hours and went back to my parents' house afterwards. That job didn't last though either. They just fired me for speaking to the visitors – apparently it wasn't my place to answer questions about what I thought about a painting.

I don't know why this always happens to me.

I had a simple dream. Nothing too ambitious. I was always smart at school and thrived on learning. I could have done great at university. It makes me so angry when I think about it. I get mad at my parents for being poor even though I know it truly isn't their fault. I get mad at my friends for going to school and sharing their experiences with me. Like they flaunt it. When I see their graduation pictures on Facebook, I just start crying. I'm already twenty years old. I should be finishing school, but I haven't even started yet. I know that I can't give up on my dream, it's what I want but sometimes it's hard and feels like a fairy tale.

Everything has its own time though. Hopefully, my time will come too.

2006
Dhaka, Bangladesh

Ramshay's Story

My marriage was done at a very young age. That's typically normal in our culture and so are dowries.

When the proposal came to my house, my father looked at the status of my now-husband and how culturally, socially and religiously similar our families were. My own family was considered lower-middle-class, so when an upper-middle-class family comes knocking on your door, you do your best to please them. It was slightly odd that they would even consider someone like me joining their family. I had very little education (I was only twelve years old) and our family was not excessively rich (we had enough to survive comfortably but not splurge). However, our values were very similar, and my husband did not mind having a first wife that was fifteen years younger than him. The only condition that his family put on ours was the dowry. They wanted a large sum of money and gifts for our home. My father agreed but later regretted it.

They had given us a sum of money to contribute towards the actual wedding day, but the dowry was much greater than we could afford. After talking to people in our community, we learnt that when they asked for 'gifts' for the couple, they expected expensive and top-quality products so that the wealth and status of the new couple could be shown off to the world. My father was able to scrape enough money together and borrow so that I could be given a respectable send-off and have the things I needed for my new home, but he could not afford the sum of money that had been agreed. After many talks between our families, my in-laws agreed to installed payments. It was not ideal but it didn't seem to cause any issues.

For two years I lived very happily. My husband was not forceful in any way and I was well respected by him and his family. That all changed when I turned fourteen. There was a constant reminder from him that my family still owed him money and when my husband lost his job, this became a priority. He continuously reminded me about the outstanding payments and would taunt me, starve me and lock me in rooms until a payment was made to him. My father tried his best, but he could not keep up with the demands, which were very different from the original payment plan.

It was one night in bed that everything changed for me.

I was waiting for my husband to get home from work. It was around midnight, and I was starting to worry as this was considerably late for him. I was lying there in our bed when I heard him stumble into the room drunk and slurring. He tried to hide a black bag from me behind the door, but I did not pay it much attention, more focused on the bandage around his hand. He shouted at me quite violently, once again reminding me that my family was indebted to him and that he was now going to take his revenge on them and me. He said that he should have never agreed to marry a child and that it was my fault because I was so alluring to him. He punched me a couple of times before he fell on the bed and went to sleep. I cried silently for a while, closing my eyes, and staying still for fear of jerking another reaction out of him. It was when the sunlight beamed through our window that I heard some shuffling from his side of the bed. The room became full of banging and noise as he pulled things from all corners. I didn't move but I thought he was sending me home to my family. I thought about how much dishonour and shame it would bring to my parents and how much people would taunt them. I was shaking inside from fear of how I was going to continue in the world with no education and a scarlet letter on my chest, but I shouldn't have been thinking so small.

Things were going to be much worse.

He pulled the blanket from on top of me and yanked me by my foot, so I was at the edge of the bed. The last thing I saw properly was a plastic bottle in his hand. I felt the liquid sting my face as if it were on fire – the sizzling of my bedsheets ringing in my ear. The pain was unbearable, and I screamed as loud as I could for help, but I felt my voice being lost in the commotion. I could hear him pull the suitcase he had packed and slam the door behind him. It all happened within seconds.

I was hospitalised for six months. I don't remember how I got to the hospital, and I don't remember when my family got there or even the police. I will never forget how hard those six months of my life were.

The hospital felt like a prison. The doctors were kind and the nurses attentive, but I felt trapped. My whole body was bandaged up so I couldn't move or do anything without a tube or my mother. I felt like I was in a cage. I felt this fleeting fear that I would never be able to do anything for myself again. I could barely hear, and my vision was severely blurred. I had operation after operation and each time they pulled back skin to heal the burns, I felt like they were chopping me up and leaving me to be killed in a slaughterhouse. I was depressed because I was in a closed room all day and all night. It was so difficult because no one understood me, but I would hear words from the news knowing I was not alone, there was just no one for me to talk to because we were all so scared. We had all just died in a way. It was also worse because my husband had fled, and he was nowhere to be found.

One of the things I remember most from my time in the hospital is when my body had recovered from the burns. My bandages were taken off and I couldn't see myself for a few moments, but I saw what other people could see of me. My doctors and my mum tried to tell me that I looked great with such conviction in their voices, but their eyes gave it away. Their eyes told me, that I would never be seen as myself ever again. When I grabbed the mirror to see myself, I screamed. I thought *Who is this? What is this? Is this me?*

It took me a long time to accept that I would have lines of moulded skin on my face. That I would have patches of discolouring where my skin was burned the most. That my nose would now be flat as there was not enough bone left to reconstruct it. It took me a while to accept that my throat would need more surgeries to help restore the vessels around my voice box and oesophagus and that I would still feel unbearable pains, but I learnt a lot. I also learnt how lucky I was to still have my sight and my ears.

Whilst recovering in hospital I discovered that there had already been over two hundred acid attacks that year alone in my country with only ten percent being convicted. I learnt that there was only one burns unit in the whole country compared to the millions of girls who needed help because they'd been victims of an acid attack.

For a while, after I left the hospital, I hid my face with shame. I felt dirty and society made me feel bad for what happened to me. Like I was not a victim but the cause of my own troubles. The things I learned at the hospital stayed with me though and I thought about how many people would be in the same position as me but unable to get the help and support I did. Moving back in with my parents after I was discharged from the hospital was like moving into a bubble of love. They didn't mollycoddle me because they wanted me to be able to move forward with my own strength and confidence, but they supported me in my healing and my transition back into my new normal.

I joined an NGO team a couple of years ago now and work to help acid attack victims. We offer a lot of support both financially and emotionally. For me, I joined to help set up more hospitals and remove the stigma. We're working with the government to remove the shame placed on women and reinforce and ensure that women are supported in rebuilding their lives without humiliation and with confidence. A lot of the work I do is in rural areas where acid attacks are a lot more common. There's a real need for support because women are so silenced here. I've worked with local doctors and financial backers to provide small hospitals with support in these rural areas. They're equipped to deal with basic acid attacks but were working on building two larger burns units in hospitals not too far away from the villages. So far with government support, the average attack of five hundred a year has been reduced to one hundred and convictions are going up, but there's a lot more work to do. It's still a problem and people still need support.

I used to be scared that my husband would come back and attack me again. The police still haven't found him, and his family claim he's no longer in the country or in contact. Now I'm not worried because I have my family, my friends and myself. I'm not the child that was sent to live with him but a woman with her own mind and powers. I'm more supported and more confident than I've ever been and I'm hoping to help other women feel that way too – even when it does feel like you've just died.

Mother Dearest
Peterborough, England

Fatimah's Story

I don't know why my mother hated me. Maybe it was because I was a girl. There was a cultural stigma against our gender. A sickness amongst people that girls carried nothing but sadness, droughts and punishment. Mum had that sickness. A sickness that you couldn't see. But she convinced me that I was sick. Everything was because of me. The miscarriages that came after me. The arguments she continuously had with my father. Her not being able to get a job. That was all on me. I was a monster.

She criticised everything. My way of eating. My way of speaking. My way of dressing. Anything that brought me joy – she would deny me it. I remember coming home one day from school – I couldn't have been more than six or seven, I was so excited because I got my first test results back and I came in the top tier of my class. She ripped the sheet out of my hands, washed away my excitement and saw the tears drop from my eyes as she ripped up the test paper into tiny little pieces – like shards of broken glass on our white tiled floor.

If I defined myself – or found even a hair of excitement in my life, she would hit me. She would find a way to take that joy from me.

I was terrified of lunch and dinner because that's when I had to face her. I spent my entire childhood alone. I just played in our garden or sat on the floor of my bedroom. My mother just made the idea of me talking to other people an anxious thought in my head – like I would fail to tell them my name. I'd try so hard to leave my body because I didn't want to be on earth anymore. To be humiliated continuously by my own mother. I felt like a ghost. I tried to hide myself. Make myself smaller but I just couldn't anymore. It all just needed to stop.

That's when the spirit fairies would come to me.

I was never afraid of them. They'd comfort me. I remember being beneath a tree at school talking to the fairies when I was about nine. Another girl asked me what game I was playing and that's when I realised nobody else could see what I was seeing. I was terrified of the world around me but when the spirit fairies were there, they sprinkle gold dust into my lungs and I would be able to breathe again for a few, blissful moments in my day. I put my big girl pants on and tried the best I could. I felt like a failure on most days, but I went to bed thankful that I could at least say I tried.

When I turned twenty, I met this magnetic force of a man at university. Maybe I was attracted to him because he provided me with a sense of security I was not afforded at home. Maybe it was because I saw silver linings in his hair and pure gold in his heart.

I don't think I'll ever quite know.

He was *that* boy though. *That* boy that everything revolved around. *That* boy who had a way with words. *That* boy with a kindness I had never felt before. I spent hours listening to him as we did lab work. I felt myself lighten when I spoke to him, and he seemed to understand my problems. He kept me behind late at university to finish a project that wasn't due for weeks because he knew I didn't want to go home. Sent me a message at night just to check I got home safely and if everything was okay.

He proposed to me on graduation day. I didn't think anything could top my first-class honours that day but when he asked me under the tree and the spirit fairies disappeared, I thought he was *that* boy that was going to change my life. I don't think there's ever been a moment in my life where I have been more wrong than I was at that moment.

It wasn't necessarily his fault. He was sick. He had mental health issues and when things got bad, I was an easy target. I should have been used to it – Mum did it to me for years. My mum always did say I was a monster. Maybe it was me that brought yet another person in my life to raise their hand at me. That floating cloud of pink cotton candy that always shined above him quickly turned into thundering showers. The magnetic force turned into a black hole that sucked precious time from our worlds.

I pushed so hard to help him. I didn't want to fail him in any way. I still feel like I owed him for giving me those few years of joy in my life. For being the monster that caused him to change so dramatically in the few months after our marriage. However, he was beyond help. We went to doctors, but he wouldn't want to tell them the extent of his condition. We went to psychologists, but he thought they were unnecessary. We went to family, but he thought I was creating an issue out of nothing.

Two children. Three trips to the hospital for 'tumbles down the stairs' 'accidental falls on my bike' or 'slipping over washing'. Four visits from social services. My husband still doesn't get it.

My six-year-old son came into my room one day and sat at the edge of my bed with a drawing in his hand. I remember staring at it and then the page was covered in drops of water. He had drawn his family and coloured me black and blue – because those were the only colours he had ever seen me in.

I sat under the tree in our garden until two that night. The spirit fairies had finally come back into my life and sprinkled some truths into my head. I didn't deserve to spend my life being a punching bag for people. Drowning in the water whilst pushing others to shore. My husband was a grown man. I could tell him to take his medicines. I could tell him when to eat his food. I could even tie his shoelaces for him. But I was not responsible for making him feel like a human being again – taking punch after punch until he finally woke up and got the help he needed.

I packed my bags and put my kids in the back of a taxi that night. Reputation. Money. Stability. None of that was worth the sacrifice of myself. What kind of a mother was I being by allowing my children to think it was normal for me to be bruised all the time? Those trips to the hospital to get stitches were normal? What kind of person was I for believing that the hurt and pain I received was because I wasn't good enough? That there was something wrong with me?

Suddenly, the world turned from black and white to colour as I sat in the car waiting for the traffic lights to change.

As bad as it was and as bad as life had been to me, I learned something about myself that night. I'm not a monster. I'm not a punishment. I'm not a drought. If anything, I'm the flood of rain that puts the fierce fires out. Where I was messing up was that I was continuing to look for happiness and security in people who had taken it away from me; I continued to give chance after chance to people who had proven that they were unworthy of them; I continued to expect a different result from someone who had no plans on changing at all. I realised, that if I could go through something like this and survive, I was already far stronger than I gave myself credit for. And if I was stronger than I seemed, then

I could take on the world and show my children what having your own piece of happiness looked like.

In Fear of My Family
Seoul, South Korea

Min's Story

I am a Muslim Revert from South Korea. I was almost seventeen years old when I reverted to Islam. It was just over a year ago now.

It was a late evening when I was on my way home from church after a bible study my parents had signed me up for. I was having faith issues already. My family are very devoted Catholics and we went to church every Sunday, but I had so many questions, so many things in my head that just didn't add up. To avoid going home, I decided to get off the bus that was heading towards my house and walk instead. I could say that my bus broke down. As I got down the road, the hustle and bustle of the town came alive. It was like an electric surge. I heard this beautiful ringing in my ears that I'd never heard before. I didn't understand a word but the way it was spoken was so poetic to me. Suddenly I became like the wind in a storm. I followed the crowd like it was normal. They stopped outside this large building and there were masses of people taking off their shoes before going in. I asked one of the elderly ladies next to me what was happening, and she asked if this was my first time. I just nodded my hand and followed her. It was the last day of Ramadhan. This community welcomed me without question. I watched as they all prayed together. It was so peaceful and then they broke their fasts. There were people who had not eaten all day, but they found it more important to give food and drink to others before even taking a sip of water for themselves. I stayed until after food. The volunteers started to box up food and I watched as they took it out of the building and loaded it up. The spare food was being donated to the Church's homeless centre.

Before I became a Muslim, I stopped believing in Christianity because there were so many questions that popped up in my head that nobody could answer. I was so close to giving up on the idea of religion. I couldn't believe that a God could be cruel to people – to leave them to starve or be in wars. I was almost on the edge of being an atheist until I found Islam that night. I saw that it was through their own choices that these people who had not eaten all day (and could have easily taken the mass of spare food home), chose to give up the rest of the food to those who needed it more. For the next three months, I went back to that mosque whenever I could. There was freedom to make your own choices there. People listened to my questions, and they gave me answers. For questions that they couldn't respond to, they simply told me to have confidence in finding my own answers because some questions, have too many options for there to be just one answer.

My family are all devout Christians. My father is especially against Islam. My dad sees it as oppressed and cult-like. He thinks that any God that can spread the message of hate through religious texts is not a God at all. I always think that if he picked up the Quran – or even just listened to those who have studied it, he would see how wrong he is. How peaceful the religion is. How liberating and free it actually is. How terrorists are only a small portion of people who have not read the book properly. There are still so many times I want to scream at him and say that the bible has also been interpreted wrong and led to acts of terror, but I don't think it's worth it. He doesn't want to understand so I really had to hide my true self from my family and everyone else – or something might have happened.

I never miss my prayers. I keep all my fasts. I read passages from the Quran every night. I really wanted to wear a scarf but refrained for the sake of my family. Eventually, though, members of my family grew curious as to why I was hiding from them- locked up in my room and going off so often (and for so long). There was one occasion when I left a family function to go and do my prayers. I think curiosity got the better of them and they decided to follow me. Everyone except my father, confronted me because they caught me praying while wearing a headscarf. They asked me if I had become a Muslim and I didn't deny it. They were so upset with me. For a few days none of them spoke to me and if they did, they only criticised and insulted me. After a while, they began to threaten me. They said they would tell my father if I didn't drop my whole Islam thing. I was petrified at that time about what my father would do, so I told them I would stop practising Islam to avoid any danger. I hid all of my religious things and would pray after everyone had slept or whenever I could – as secretly as I could. I was a criminal in my home, but it didn't feel like home anymore because I was ostracised. After everything that happened, my faith is what got me through it.

What my family do not understand is that I haven't been brainwashed. No one found me. No one forced me. I found myself and I've never been this happy. I've studied and searched for answers myself and now I feel complete. My faith answered all of my questions and restored a lot of the hope I had lost in the world.

Moving away for university is the only time I am free to truly express myself. I finally got to start wearing my headscarf. It wasn't easy for me as it is my first time wearing it in front of everyone and people made odd comments because I was different, but they grew not to care about my appearance. They liked me. My values. Every time I go home, I still have to take it off though. Some of my family know I've changed, but my mother asked me to spare my father. He's near the end of his days on this earth and she doesn't want his view of me being tainted. If only they could understand.

I am so happy. I am so free.

My Mother Did It for Me
Berlin, Germany

Maria's Story

My father was a deadbeat. I was raised by my mum with some help from my grandfather.

It wasn't the easiest childhood, but I had a great one. My mum looked for a lot of jobs and ended up working for a production company. They weren't the most convenient hours for a single mum, but it was the only job she interviewed for and got. She took it knowing that there was some support from my grandfather, otherwise, it wasn't ideal for her. My grandad would take me to school in the morning and then afterwards drop me off to my mum at work. She was one of the lead actresses in the play.

I was fascinated by everything there.

The colours, the production. I was a wide-eyed Bambi. For my mum it was hard. Most of the time production ran late and she would feel so bad taking me home at ten o'clock at night. She felt the strain when I asked her to help me do my maths homework, but she had to rehearse for the show that night. It was difficult for her but the people there became like a second family to me. Each production went on for about six months. Over that time, I got to sit with the writers, the director and the design team. I got to see so much and got so much help. The scriptwriters helped me with my reading – getting me to practice the scripts. The finance department helped me with my maths homework during their breaks and my class projects were one of the best thanks to the design department.

There were days I was upset. My friends were travelling around the world or to adventure theme parks, but we didn't have the money for extra curriculum activities. On days I felt down because a friend of mine went on holiday somewhere, the costume department would bring me an outfit and props so I could have a holiday of my own. No matter where I said, they would make it come to me. I was probably the most travelled five-year-old when I thought about it like that.

I think the best memory I have is that I had my own seat in the theatre during rehearsals and run throughs. I wasn't meant to but whenever there was a coffee break, I would go up to all the actors and critique their skills. Me, a five-year-old, telling professionals where they were going wrong. I loved the theatre.

My mum worked there for five years in a range of productions. The money wasn't much, but it let us survive. We ate out of tins and packets a lot – especially after my grandfather died. Spaghetti hoops were probably my favourite. Sometimes the lady across the road would look after me when my mum had a show in the evening, and it would run too late. The theatre shows took a lot of commitment, but they let my mum still be my mum.

The years were hard on her though and every penny that came into her pocket seemed to just fall out. She was worn down a lot by the hours at the theatre, but she never let it show. On her days off, we would be at the park or go swimming.

When I was seventeen, I had left some university leaflets out on the table. They had been given to me by my school, but I had no intention of going. We didn't have the money. My mum and I spoke about it at great length, and I told her what I would have done if I could go but that I was okay. It wasn't that important to me. The next morning, I woke up to see the form filled and a check for my first year of education.

She raised me on her own. When I graduated with a first in my English and Journalism degree last year, I saw it more as her accomplishment than mine.

The Path
São Paulo, Brazil

Clara's Story

My husband and I came from the same community. Both of us watched our parents struggle with finances.

That's what drew me to my husband when we first met. He went out and hustled on the streets every day. He worked any job he could find – cleaning cars, shop floors or the streets. He wanted to improve his life despite the difficult start he was given.

We bonded one night after he saw me walking down the street around one in the morning. He said this was no time for any lady to be out, but I told him I needed to escape. My mum and dad argued all the time over money. My dad was a bad alcoholic and things got violent in my house. My little brother could sleep through anything, but I couldn't. I found it difficult to be around. That night was the start of our relationship. We dated for four years before he proposed to me under the streetlamp he found me under that very first night we first spoke properly.

After twenty years of marriage, I caught my husband cheating and had to leave him. A lot of my family said to not be so silly. Think of your children. How is a woman your age going to survive? What prospects do you have? I just couldn't put up with it. Every time he went to work or looked at his phone, I just thought he was going to be with someone else. Talk to someone else. I didn't want to live my life always wondering what he was doing – even if he really was doing something innocent. The trust had been broken.

Honestly, I wish I'd gotten my divorce much sooner.

For so long I'd been denying myself the right to be an individual. When I became a wife, I put the needs of my husband first. When I had children, they consumed everything I did. The family had become so much more important than my dreams. I don't regret my decisions. Watching my children grow up was magical. I was there for all their first milestones. Steps, words and loves. I had small joys: Getting a brand-new car, having our twentieth anniversary, my son getting into college.

Now, the pleasures I enjoy are much greater. More intense. I'm doing all the things I love to do with no one telling me that I can't because I have to commit to my family. I studied nutrition and got a job at the hospital. I buy whatever I want, whenever I want. I watch cartoons without being called a child. I never miss a Disney movie. I go to the ballet at least once a month. Right now I'm coming back from a class on finance. I'm going to invest in the stock market and get a house by the beach.

My children are so supportive of me. I'm not a burden on them or myself. I have no limits.

Against the Odds
Harrow, England

Amelia's Story

I've always wanted to be a lawyer. There's not a single moment in time that I can remember wanting to be anything else. It was all the programmes I saw on TV. My mum used to watch them after she put me to bed, and I would watch them from the corridor – hiding behind the cloth covering our pantry.

It was difficult when I was young. We were still living in a fairly new world. Girls were only just beginning to leave the patriarchal thoughts behind and begin venturing out into the world completely by themselves.

Telling my careers support teacher, Mrs Brown, at college what I wanted to be was quite the experience. I remember her asking me if I was sure. She said, "Millie this is a very big commitment. Are you sure you want to study so hard to sit at home?"

My blood boiled for a short while, but I didn't reply to her. The best thing for me was to show everyone they were wrong. I made my application without telling anyone but my dad. I didn't want to get my hopes up and although my father was a realist, he was very supportive of me.

It had been three months before I got any letters back. The first two were rejections. It deflated my little bubble of hope. It made me question whether I'd made the right decision or if I'd just been stupid to risk so much on my dream. It took six months before I heard anything from any other universities but out of my five choices, I got two acceptances and one where I had to take one final test. Despite having to take an additional test, it was that university that I wanted to be at.

When I arrived for my test, I was really nervous. I had found out one of my other friends, Bridgette, was going so we made the journey there together but didn't dare speak. We kept questioning what would be on the test. What the university would look like. Would our big adventure be everything we'd heard?

The law school admissions test was in a big classroom. Bridgette and I were the only women in the room. To say I was now nervous would have been an understatement. I was bouncing in my seat like a caffeinated squirrel. I wasn't sure how the test would go or if I'd even do well.

Whilst I was sat there waiting for the test to start, I felt timid. I sort of made myself smaller, sinking into my seat so I was out of sight of the guys, but it didn't make a difference. A group of boys started yelling things at Bridgette and me like, "you don't need to be here," "there's plenty else you can do," and "you'll always have a job in my kitchen if this doesn't work out." It turned into a pile on. The boys tried to get in my head. Some of them even went as far as to guilt us into dropping out there and then.

It was intense.

I couldn't afford to lose focus though. I also had something to lose if I didn't do well. I didn't want to mess up this test or this opportunity I had been given, so I kept my head down. I didn't look around this massive room at all of the boys. I didn't even look at my friend Bridgette next to me. I just kept my head down until the examiner came in to tell us we could begin.

To many people, I looked cold, unemotional, or even a little bit stupid. It was an ambitious move for a woman to even apply for university, but to apply to such a university and not give a damn about other people's opinions – that woman was dangerous. However, I learnt very quickly at a young age that a woman needed to control her emotions if she was going to make it in a man's world. If I broke down or lost my temper, it would be blamed on my gender not because society was unjust. It was – and often still is, a hard path to walk but it has to be done because as harsh as it feels, it also protects you and keeps you steady for the next fight.

There have been many times in my life that I've been seen as cold. People have said that I've been walled off at university or work, but I know I'm not like that. I don't see myself like that. My friends don't see me like that. My family definitely don't see me like that.

I ended up passing that test and spent four years at Oxford University as one of only ten girls in my year. There were roughly one hundred and eighty boys. My entire time there, the boys tried to make it difficult for me. They gave me the runt of the work if we had group projects. They tried to get me to quit but I refused to. My parents were so proud of me. I was so proud of myself. I wasn't giving up being a lawyer for anyone.

When I graduated, I worked in an office in London. I learnt there that childish behaviour does not end after university but only continues. I'll tell you something. Women are considered fragile, but I've never seen anything as easily wounded as a man's ego. Men and their emotions.

I was treated more as a secretary than a lawyer. I was often given cases last minute and would pull all-nighters trying to get the evidence and case put together. Once all the work had been done, my case would be given to some male to present in a courtroom.

I presented my first case in a courtroom after three years of working at my firm. It was only because my male colleague got ill, and we had to be in the courtroom in thirty minutes. I was the only person who knew the case. I walked out of the courtroom victorious. The thrill I felt whilst I was presenting my case, it was nothing like I had experienced before. I knew I wanted to do this for the rest of my life but that would not be possible there. At that firm.

I applied for loads of other jobs and got one at a smaller firm not too far from where I worked. It was actually suggested to me by a man on the train one day. It was the perfect fit. I practised the law I saw on TV – the type that actually made it into a courtroom with more than thirty minutes' notice. I wasn't made to feel like less but like an equal. I practised there for over ten years. When I left, I left as a junior partner. I won over seventy cases and only lost ten. I worked on everything from petty theft to a double manslaughter charge. The jobs have been tough, but I've loved every minute of it.

For the past forty-five years, I've been the main partner at my own law firm in London. We've worked towards equal opportunities for women in the workplace and ensured that we are not a minority in my workplace (and hopefully others). Each year we use our bonuses to pay for at least ten girls studying Law from different universities in the UK to get a full scholarship. I've got a great family but even they've felt the strain of my work, so I've started to pull back on my cases. I mainly focus on cases involving women now and do a lot of pro-bono cases.

This is the law that I wanted to practise. No boundaries. No bias. Just law.

The Night She Changed Me
Lahore, Pakistan

Bushra's Story

I left an abusive relationship. For years I put up with it. My husband often taunted me for being barren. We had been married for over ten years and had struggled to conceive a child. His mother made the situation worse. Often after conversations with her, my husband would come and punch me in the stomach. It wasn't my mother-in-law's fault either. Our community liked to taunt her and then her, me.

After a lot of praying to God, I fell pregnant and went for my first scan. The doctor took me to the side, away from my husband, and asked me how many times I had miscarried. I told her none, but she was insistent. She said that I needed to be honest with her because she could see in the scan that some damage had been done to my uterus and this could affect my baby. That night changed me. My husband and his family were happy for a short amount of time when we got home from the scan but that did not last. He quickly turned back to his abusive self, and no one tried to protect my baby. As my child grew every day, I knew I had to protect them.

I had found out the sex of my baby at the beginning of my pregnancy. My husband's family were sure it would be a boy. I did not tell them it was a girl. I was scared of what they would do to her. Once she was born, his family started to make comments. Now that I was no longer barren, I was shaming them with a daughter for a first child. The mithai (Pakistani sweets) they had initially ordered with excitement were now handed out in our community with saddened faces. When I got home from the hospital – only giving birth 24 hours earlier, they expected me to return to all my household work and care for my daughter at the same time. No one helped me. My husband just got angry every time he saw our daughter and would hit me. It was my fault she was a girl.

I knew I wanted more for her than my family wanted for me. I was married to the first family that came to our home asking for my hand in marriage. My father could not afford to keep all of us and, as I was the only girl, wanted me to get married first. My husband's family did not ask for a dowry and because of this, my father set a wedding date before they left.

In the morning after prayers, I left with my daughter. It was hard. I had nowhere to go, and society is still not forgiving.

I have Hepatitis C which was caused by the many blood transfusions I needed when I was in labour. Due to the hepatitis, no one was willing to take me in when I first left my husband's home. I begged many people, but no one would help. I got far away from my husband and his family. I spent many nights on the streets. I don't know how long I will live.

Looking into my daughter's eyes, I saw something special in her. I tried to give her up for adoption so that she'd have a good home and the chance to have more than I could ever provide for her. I met a few women and the wife of a minister told me about a place where I could drop her off. I dressed her in her best dress and packed all of her favourite things. I held her tight but when I got there, I just couldn't bring myself to do it.

Everything I did now was because I wanted her to have the best. I'm trying to help her figure out her future.

I started working at the Sunday market, and I asked this man for help setting up a stand of my own. I didn't know much about shops but enough to get me by and have now been doing it for a few weeks. Some people make comments, particularly the men, but I don't care. I look at my daughter and I know I'm doing my best. Many women come to my stall but I'm still trying to learn how to run my shop.

I met a young man when I first started. I told him about my story and showed him my bruises and marks. He has tried to help me as much as he can, but his means are limited. His own income is only 2500 rupees a week and he's getting engaged next week. He's trying to set up a committee to donate blood because I really need it. He's done so much to help me and I'm now starting to get the right medical advice. Even if I cannot win my battle, I will die knowing I did the best for my daughter. She'll know her mother did not give up on her.

Doe-Eyed Girls
Malé, Maldives

Fiona's Story

I want to start by saying I love my daughter very much. She is beautiful and confident but sometimes she is stupid.

Her father has always left situations surrounding her love life to me. She has a big heart, but she lets everyone abuse it. I've told her to be tougher but one tug on her heartstring and they can play the whole symphony.

Over the years she's had a couple of boyfriends. I tried to warn her about her last boyfriend, but she didn't want to listen. My daughter is very headstrong. She thinks she knows but she knows deep down that's not true.

She always starts doe-eyed in any relationship. She thinks these men can move the stars in the sky. Society had originally women think the sun did not rise without the command of a man. So, it's not entirely her fault. But I raised her better. She never realises that she is the star. She does not need to move anywhere – just shine.

Once I overheard her last boyfriend telling her that she needed to respect him. I thought I'd taught her to value her self-worth more. If she listened to me more as a little girl, rather than sulk maybe she'd remember these important lessons – not just what song was on the radio or what actor was on the TV. I knew that he was bad news. I tried to warn her, but she did not want to listen. She was in her own little bubble.

Then he left his home because he got into an argument with his family. I remember her being on the phone after he walked out. She was so worried about where he would go. How he would look after himself. How his family could do something like that to him. Something clicked in me that night. I told her, "If he'll do that to his family, he'll do it to you too." I wanted her to realise that this boy thinks everything is disposable. If he could leave the woman who birthed and raised him, how could you trust he won't leave a woman he has known for only six months?

She didn't listen.

She stopped talking to me for a long time. It bothered me in the beginning. I couldn't understand how this little girl that I had raised tirelessly with so much love and affection, could just stop talking to me. I quickly got over these feelings. I knew she needed time to go through this. If she did not learn for herself now, there wouldn't be any chance. I couldn't walk her through everything in life.

One night, there was a knock on our door. It was very late, and we were not expecting anyone. My husband went to answer the door and returned quickly to our bedroom. Behind him stood my daughter with a bouquet of yellow roses. My favourite. Sure enough, he took off and left her. She came back and thanked me. She hasn't made any mistakes like that since then.

Go on, tell them. Mama was right.

Stepping Up
Queens, New York, USA

Trina's Story

I was eleven when my mum divorced my stepdad. She had four kids at the time, and I remember wondering how we were going to cope. My mum did not work, and we had nowhere to go. I knew it was the right move though. My stepdad worked and provided for us, but he was not a nice man. He frequently belittled us and continuously put my mum down. She was on the verge on a breakdown when we left.

We moved in with some of our relatives for a few months. The five of us lived in a small, boxed room. My mum worked two jobs. She worked a carer during the day, helping elderly people in our area. At night, she worked at a fast-food restaurant. She scrimped and saved. We all moved to a nice house not too far away from our distant family. It wasn't as big as the one we had when we lived with my stepdad, but we were all happy. Mum's health was significantly better, and we all knew our role. Mum got longer shifts at her care centre and her pay increased. We were never rich. We didn't have the same amount of money coming in as when we lived with my stepdad, but we were comfortable. We were happy and we were safe.

Sitting in my bedroom one day before she left my stepdad, I remember she said to me, "You're the oldest so I'm going to need your help now." Ever since then, I've been 'Mum Number Two'.

A routine quickly built in my life. I picked my little brothers up from school. I cooked for them. It would have been basic as my cooking wasn't very good, but it was still food. I made sure they did their homework and helped them whenever they were stuck. I met with their teachers. I'd be the authority figure until Mum came home from work at seven. After we all had dinner, I would go to focus on my studies. I wanted to study. I wanted to go to university. I had my own ambitions and I just felt I needed to work on how to balance my family with them.

I was always the responsible one. Nobody ever had to worry about me. Now I'm twenty and my whole life has been about my little brothers. I let them take over my life, so they didn't take over my mum's. I've never really felt the security to figure myself out. I did well at school, but I struggled to pick a college that was flexible around my family at the time.

I took a year out to figure myself out. I made myself a priority. I got a job in my little brother's school as a nursery class helper. I enjoyed my experience, but I learned I didn't want to work with kids from it. My brothers and I bonded over the year. They were older and saw me less as their mother and more as their sister. I was still there to feed them, take them to school and help them with their homework but they felt more comfortable telling me the mischievous things they got up. They worried less about me telling them off and more about what fun activity we could do. We spent most of our Friday afternoons getting milkshakes after they finished school. It was our treat.

Today is orientation at my new college. I just finished meeting with my advisor. There are so many clubs and organisations that I can join. I want to meet a lot of different people. I want to be more outspoken. I feel like this is my chance to learn who I am without worrying about how my decision is going to affect my family. I just need to think about myself.

A Battle with Anxiety
Alexandria, Egypt

Lana's Story

He always wanted a daughter. My baba tells me that all the time.

Egyptian people are still clinging to our old culture in that way. Either they don't want daughters, or they want their daughter to do their housework, educate themselves to just become mothers and stay…innocent. There's nothing wrong with it. My mum did that and she's amazing, but times are changing. Girls don't want to be like Stepford wives. They want to go out and change their little corner of the world.

My friends think I'm so lucky because a lot of their dads aren't affectionate. My baba really wanted a girl even though his family and friends kept telling him how expensive we are. They say girls are only yours until they are married – then they are someone else's. We're still seen to many men as property – just with a little more wiggle room to decorate ourselves. My baba let me be free. Some of my friends have even been forced to stop studying and get married but my baba wants me to be successful. He wants me to live abroad. More than anything, he's my friend.

I don't know why but most of the time that wasn't enough for me. I crumbled under the idea that I had to be perfect all the time. Appearance. Behaviour. Education. Maybe it was because my parents gave me such freedoms.

I didn't want people to turn around and say to them, "this is what happens when you give a girl too much – she becomes useless."

There was a time in high school when I was extremely depressed. Mostly just teenage things but my mind played devil's advocate. I felt ugly. I didn't have any confidence. I began to crumble on the inside, and it got so bad that I started having scary thoughts. I constantly felt like everyone was laughing behind my back. I constantly felt like I was…drowning under a pile of bricks.

I didn't want to tell anyone, especially my parents. I was partially afraid I'd get locked away in the house, but I was also afraid of upsetting them. It got so bad though that one night we were sitting in my bedroom, and I finally let my baba know. I was terrified of how he would react. Most of my friends hide their feelings from their families. People don't understand mental health. People don't really understand human emotion. Most of my friends always made fun of people who became depressed or had anxiety because they thought it was just mind over matter. I didn't want to be mocked like that because I felt this was greater than that. It was more painful.

Baba's reaction wasn't what I expected. He didn't panic or scream. He was calm. He just kept holding me and saying, "We'll get through this together."

Which we did.

After seeing a therapist and openly talking at the dinner table, my mind began to ease itself. No matter how stupid I thought I felt or how low I got, my family supported me. I never felt like an outcast. There are still days I feel low, and I still have a long way to go but I'm doing better. I'm keeping myself open. I have safe people I can talk to about my thoughts, and I think that helps the most. I'm much better than I was three years ago.

I'm at university at the moment trying to understand myself better. I've started a degree in psychology. There's no such thing as a wrong thought or idea there. I'm constantly growing. Every evening I tell my baba about what I've learnt, and he just watches me glow up. I think – I hope that he is proud of me.

One day, I'm hoping to gain enough confidence to campaign about mental health here in Egypt. We need to change perceptions. My kitchen is as far as I can go at the moment but I'm sure I'll get there. One day.

Living to Escape
Abidjan, Ivory Coast

May's Story

I grew up on a farm. We had two cows, five chickens, one horse and three sheep. We got a couple of goats by the time I turned five. We used to help my father cultivate the land. It was hard work. The ground was always very dry, and our closest water well was about a twenty-minute walk away but we managed to live off what we made.

We were really poor as a family when I was little. My father worked really hard but there were these men that would come and loot us every month. They would take all the money my mum would have saved. If we did not comply, they would retaliate. Once they burnt our horse's stable. We managed to save our horse but lost a lot of seeds and crops. Another time, they beat my father up for not giving them the money fast enough. I hated watching him from behind the griddle window of our house but there was nothing I could do.

There was this time that I was playing outside in the crop fields with my little brother. We didn't have much money, but those people never took away our spirit. My brother and I laughed hysterically as we ran through the greening crops-the leaves hiding our faces as we hunted for one another in a game of hide and seek.

That's when everything changed.

I was looking for my brother when these men turned up. There were about six of them, all wearing these black masks over their mouths. I called out to my brother before running into the house to get my dad. Whenever these men came, I was usually told to hide in my bedroom. This was the first time they'd seen me. They had come a few days early for their money. When I got inside, my mum held me tight. She could hear the shouting from outside and tried her best to cover my ears. The men were speaking in a dialect I did not understand but I remember my mum. She fell to the ground and then I heard a gunshot.

Trying my best, I managed to get my mum to regain consciousness. I could hear my dad screaming from outside, but I prioritised my mum. She was completely out of it. When she was fine, I went outside to see my little brother sitting next to my dad. There was a gunshot wound to his left leg. I applied pressure to it and then bandaged it up – just like I had seen some medics who came to our village do a few times over the years. He wouldn't stop sobbing. He kept apologising. I didn't understand it.

The next day the men came back. My mum started wailing as soon as she heard their tyres coming to a screeching halt and locked herself in her bedroom. My little brother had been sent to a friend's house earlier so was nowhere in sight. My dad grabbed my arm and placed a silver bangle on it. He told me he had crafted it himself and he never wanted me to take it off.

"Be brave now, my child, and know we really had no choice. I failed to protect you. They'd have killed us all and still taken you if I put up a fight."

My mouth dropped as soon as he finished his sentence. I couldn't speak and I didn't have the chance. I felt these arms grip around my waist and my feet heavy above the ground. One minute I was in my house hallway and the next I was tied and sitting in the back of a black army style car. Three men who just stared at me the entire time. The rest became a blur.

I was a baby when I got married. I was only thirteen. I didn't have an adolescence. One day I was playing in the fields with children my age and the next day I'm a mother. Responsible for a home and other people.

I cried so much.

The men took me miles away from my village. My family. The journey was overnight, and we ended up outside a mansion, where an auction was being held. There were many girls like me at the auction. Some looked older but they were mostly around my age. I was sold to the person I married at the auction. I knew nothing about him, and he knew nothing about me.

My husband turned out to be a cold man. He had zero communication or understanding. He treated me like an animal. There were days I would not eat any food because he felt like depriving me. There were days he used me as a punching bag. I suffered for so long, but I endured it all so that I could raise my children well. I knew I could not take my children away from the luxuries that he could provide for them in his large stately home.

Every human has a ceiling though and once you hit it, it's over.

For three years I planned my escape. I learned my husband's schedule. Where he went and for how long. On which days he worked late. Which days he'd stay on the grounds of the property. I learnt all the routes around the land, where there were safe spaces and where I could go to not be found. I thought about it a lot, but I knew that my only way to be truly free was through the law. I was not a convict. I did not want to hide all my life. I waited until my children were older.

One morning I left the keys on the table, dropped my kids off at school, and headed straight for the courts. It took a couple of hours but when it was done, I felt a great weight being lifted off my shoulder. I took my children out of school early that day and we drove overnight to our new home.

I finally have freedom. I'm laid back. I'm relaxed. I can express my opinion. I do whatever I want. I just finished a wonderful vacation in Egypt with my daughter. Nobody causes me trouble anymore.

These are the best years of my life.

The Aftermath
Chittagong, Bangladesh

Samiha's Story

I was born without a zip on my mouth – free to spiel whatever thoughts that came to my brain without having to fear the repercussions.

My family always told me to voice my opinions to them. They taught me that honesty does not forego kindness but that the two are interlinked and that my honesty must come with kindness and compassion. Whenever I had to say any opinion, I always said it in the kindest, most honest way possible. I did not want to have to bow to something I did not agree with, but I also never wanted to hurt someone's feelings.

This was something that stayed on my mind every time a proposal came to my house. I wanted to be kind to them as they had gone to the effort of coming to my house with gifts and sweet treats, but I did not want to say yes to someone who I could not see myself, spending the rest of my life with.

I was walking home from college one day when a man on his motorbike stopped me. He had followed me from the college gates to my bus stop just up the road and made me feel a little bit uncomfortable – especially when he tried to speak to me. I tried my best to ignore him, but his flirting was persistent. He kept complimenting my looks, saying that I was hypnotising and must have had all the boys lining up behind me. He said, "you'll need a real man like me to protect you." I told him that I don't want a boyfriend and that all proposal prospects went through my mother and father first. I told him that I was sorry, but I could not do anything without my parent's approval first.

I thought that was the end of the conversation but somehow, he ended up at my house the next evening asking my father for my hand in marriage.

My parents pulled me into the kitchen to ask for my opinion. I could tell they did not like the boy. His greasy hair and specific smell just emphasised that he was still 'looking for the right job' and wasted his day away smoking and drinking. I didn't want that for myself and neither did my parents, so we politely declined and made our excuses. We could tell he was not taking the rejection well through his brass gestures of anger, but we did not think the matter would go any further. Many people who had come would leave angry because they felt like we had wasted their time, but they later understood that we just weren't a good match. We hoped this would be the same.

The next day I was walking towards my bus stop. My scarf was loosely over my head, and I was in a rush to get home. It was the day my favourite drama came on so I needed to get all my work done as quickly as possible so I would be free to watch it. I heard a beeping come from behind me and I turned my head to see if it was my bus that was approaching. As I turned, I felt my hair being grabbed from behind me and this liquid was hurled in my face. It stung as I shrieked out for help. I could hear him screaming – the greasy haired man, "Now let's see who will marry you."

A lot of people ran to help me, and they kept throwing things over me to try and help. We tried everything from water to milk but nothing helped to stop the pain I was feeling. The acid burned and I felt it seep its way through my skin until the doctor at the hospital put me to sleep.

The acid left my face disfigured. My eyesight became permanently blurred and the entire left side of my body – from my head to my hand, needed to be treated for burns. I had to have ten operations and now have to go back yearly. I was left traumatised.

It was fortunate that the events happened at a busy time. We were lucky that he got convicted. The police tracked him down easily and threw everything they could at him. My abuse did not stop when he went to prison though. As well as having to learn to navigate my life in the shadows of shame, my family and I were sent a lot of death threats. He had people throw flaming bottles at our house. I got letters sent to me saying that I would be beheaded upon his release in thirty years and that my whole family and I would be left alone. My family felt extremely unsettled, and I struggled to come to terms with how I looked. How I could not see well. How I could not do many things.

We decided as a family to pack what we had left after a fire burnt a portion of our house. We moved to a city over five hours away from us with the help of the people in our community. It was hard because our whole lives were there, but we couldn't do it. We had to become new people and have a new life.

Moving has been the best thing that happened to me.

When we first moved, I hid in my room. I would only leave the house when I needed to and even then, I was covered from head to toe. All people would see were my eyes. However, I met a lot of women in our new community that had struggled. Many of them left domestic abuse and although they did not the pain I had felt, they sympathised with the aftermath. The emotions I felt. The trap I led myself to believe I was in. These women helped my family integrate themselves into society with confidence and honour. They helped me get a job as a tutor. I was really good at math and wanted to pursue it before everything happened. They helped me find my passion for it again. I'm also getting married in a month to the kindest and most honest person I've ever met. He is a young man who works as a mechanic. He's the nephew of one of the ladies whose children I mentor. He's seen all my scars and knows that I can't see very well but he accepts it all because we can talk properly. We can have conversations about books and theories. We can talk about what the world has to offer.

Every now and then, I think about that boy in prison. I wonder if he'll ever find me and sometimes, I'm paranoid enough to think he's close to it. I then remember that there's still another twenty-six years until he is realised and that he is far, far away. I'm in a community now where we're all like family and they have my back.

I must now live my life for myself as myself.

Watching the Clock Tick by Five Times
London, England

Hannah's Story

My mindset hadn't changed since I was a child. I always knew then, what I still know now. I wanted a large family and I wanted to be at home to raise them. That's what I wanted. Not because I was told or taught I wanted it. Not because that's all I had seen on the television or read in the books. I wanted to do it because I knew what it was like not to have it. Not to have either parent at home whenever I had an issue or just wanted to talk. I wanted to be there for them. I wanted to be reliable.

Life as a child was busy. I was one of five siblings. My parents had moved to England before I was even born, and they fought to show they had a right to be here. To be seen as more than just immigrants taking British jobs. My mum and dad worked all hours of the day to provide for us. To give us the best they could. We had the best education, at the best schools. As a result, though, they were gone in the mornings and afternoons. When they came home in the evenings, tired and worn, my mum would head straight into the kitchen to make dinner and my dad would get on with whatever tasks he had in the house. My parents worked incredibly hard for all five of us, but I barely saw them. When they both passed away, I was only fifteen. My dad passed away when I wasn't there and I watched my mum fight breast cancer. Those days that she was in the hospital and at home, were probably the days I spent the most time with her, but even then, she did not want to stop. She wanted us to have as much as possible. To make sure we were comfortable.

Both of my parents left me with freckles of memories but a lot of what they did were always filled in by uncles. I knew of my parents, but I did not know them. I did not remember them the way I wanted. So, I decided that my children would have it differently. They're small moments but I do remember them. I was watching the new Dallas with my daughter once and I remembered my mum. The heartbreak she had when they killed Bobby off for one whole season. It was the only programme I remember my mum sitting down to watch. I remember sitting with my mum just like I did with my daughter.

Those are the types of memories I'm building with my kids. Small ones but memorable ones and many of them.

After my parent's death, my life was scattered around my brothers and then university. I did a degree at my grandfather's insistence because I didn't have anything that I particularly wanted to do, and he was so passionate. He wanted me to move back to my parent's homeland and get a government job. I didn't think too much about later, I just got on with my degree.

University was probably one of the loneliest times of my life. One of my brothers said living away would be a wild and fun adventure. For me, it was just hollow. I missed my young nieces who filled my days with laughter. I missed family contact and writing a letter just wasn't the same. I had people around me all day, but I craved the comforts of my home. It was funny because I didn't really have a home at the time. I stayed in the university dorms, or I stayed at my oldest brother's house but my family there were home to me. I just wanted to be closer to them. The final year of my degree was probably my happiest. I stayed in my parents' house by myself. There was a different kind of comfort there. The commute to university was long but worth it. I was close to my family and close friends. I had people I enjoyed spending my free time with and I was within my comfort zone.

I finished my degree in the end. I didn't particularly enjoy it, nor did I see it as particularly useful to me, but I still had one. Just in case I ever needed it.

Then I got married. I moved back to my parent's homeland. I was always told from a young age that I would marry someone from back home, so I did, and I was happy to. Life there wasn't what I had expected. It was difficult and at times frustrating, but I got on with it. I had two children – coming back and forth from there to England and then back. Life was difficult but my children made me happy. Just being with them was enough.

As time passed, life changed. We moved as a family to England and then to London. My husband worked as long as he was being watched but when we moved to London, he became lazier. My words were lost in his ears, and I had to start picking up where I could. I now had three children and my focus was on being a mother, so I managed the best I could. That was the thing. People started to make comments. People were disappointed that I didn't use my degree. Comments were made about how my parent's made sacrifices for me to be educated so I could provide for my family, but I didn't want to provide for my children in just the money sense. I provided for my children in a way I thought and still do think, was better. I created memories with them. I enriched them with trips out and days with their cousins. I went to all their assemblies and took them for days in the parks. On days they were sick, I would pick them up from school and nurse them back to health. I did every school drop off and pick. They knew they could come to me with a problem at any hour – although I did miss my sleep in the middle of the night when they turned up or were coughing their guts out.

Eventually, after four children and one miscarriage, my marriage deteriorated. It wasn't brilliant for a while, but I wanted my children to know their father. To see I gave it every chance I could. That as their mother, I tried for them. When I separated, my youngest was only four and all my children were still in education. I had to be a grown-up and my dream of staying with them was dashed. I had to get a job. I had to be the breadwinner. That changed a lot for me and gave me a lot of guilt.

My older three children had me for everything. Assemblies, Christmas productions, school trips, parent's evening or when they were ill. My youngest daughter now had to relinquish that as it became more difficult to attend all these things and work. She would ask me to help out at her school and I would always have to say, "I'll try my best, but I might have to work then." I'm grateful for the job I had then. It helped my family out so much when we needed it the most, but I missed things. There were times my youngest would stop asking me to come to things or take her to things because she knew the answer. It's been difficult but all my children have grown and understand.

I've changed jobs now and try and fit all my holidays around my kids but still don't enjoy working. I'm good at my job and have had my boss and colleagues praise me many times but I don't thrive with work. I thrive with my kids. I'm still trying to get a balance between work life and home, although I am still hoping that one of my older ones will start earning big bucks so I can just stay at home soon.

People still make comments today to me about working, my degree and my life choices. Some of them I may agree with, but I've never regretted spending so much time with my kids or having any of my children. Being a homemaker as opposed to a working woman. We may have lived less lavishly than most of my family and friends and some of my children may still see that as a more glamourous life, but I learnt the value of money years ago. When they're older, I think they'll understand too. We can earn money at any point in our life. We can always get that back. However, memories cannot be brought with money but only made with time and that's something we can never get back once it's gone.

Life has thrown me many curveballs. People have seen me in all shades of black, white and blue. Life has certainly made me into a coloured canvas. However, during my time with my children, the memories and time we've spent together, my children have always painted me golden.

Will This Be Just Another Dream?
Erbil, Iraq

Inziya's Story

We live in a very conservative culture, but I want my children to be open-minded.

I was brought up to feel like my ideas were wrong. I was brought up on the silent idea that some people are better than others based on their skin tone or their gender. I was brought up being told there were different rules for girls than for boys. It was difficult because I had many dreams. So many big ideas. I thought they were the start of something amazing, but I quickly realised they would just be one more dream that I could not make come true.

When I got married, I made a very conscious decision to raise my children without restriction. I wanted them to have their own stories to tell. I wanted them to have passions and dreams. I try to bring them to as many places as possible. Big shopping centres, art galleries, concerts. My husband and I want them to see as many types of people as possible and as many types of ideas as possible. We want them to see that nothing stops at your gender or skin tone or religion. Everything just starts with one spark in your brain.

Who knows, maybe this could be the start of something wonderful.

In the Moonlight
Rio de Janeiro, Brazil

Alessandra's Story

I didn't enjoy life very much because I was always sacrificing for the future.

My whole life has been about studying and working. I worked so many jobs so that I could save money. I went to college. I got my MBA. I didn't travel very much because I didn't have the time or the funds. I didn't get married. I didn't have kids. All I wanted to do was feel secure. I grew up in great uncertainty. I didn't even know if my mum was going to make it through her cancer treatment. We moved house a lot because we kept getting evicted. My dad would go for weeks at a time to work on some jobs he'd been offered. This left me to look after my mum, but she slept most of the time – sometimes so much that I thought she'd died. The uncertainty used to drive me crazy. Would I have parents tomorrow? Would I have a roof over my head next week? Would I be able to attend my school lessons?

I've had bad mental health problems my entire life. I didn't really recognise it as a child but as I grew older and saw the doctor more regularly, they told me I needed to start treatment. I get really bad anxiety and am severely depressed. People here don't understand mental health, but it's stopped me from doing a lot. I'm always afraid that if I stop working for even a minute, I'll end up back in my slum. If I don't pay my health bill, I'll end up with terminal cancer like my mum.

For a few years, my mental health got so bad that I couldn't save. I lost my job because I kept having panic attacks at work and they said I was wasting their time. The job market is brutal when you're my age. People didn't think I could learn new things. Most of the time, they still don't. I couldn't even get work as a clerk because they think I'm overqualified. I had no money. I could barely afford food and transportation. I spent one evening walking along the water. It was dark that night and I just wanted to dip my foot in. The water was freezing. My foot turned into my leg, my leg turned into my waist and my waist into my neck. I floated in the water for a bit as the moonlight shone brightly on my face. I heard the waves crash against my ear and a soft murmur in the sea. In that moment, I felt like nothing else could be this perfect. I didn't think about the fact that I was broke or homeless. I was transfixed by the rhythm of the sea. So I put my head under and let myself sink.

I woke up the next morning hooked to five different medications and a few machines. The lights blurred my vision, but I think I remember I saw an angel when I opened my eyes. The room smelt like fresh lemons and the white blur seemed safe. When I regained full consciousness, the doctor told me they had to keep me under observation because I had tried to kill myself. I didn't remember trying to die and whilst I sat in my hospital bed, I came to realise that I didn't want to die. I just wanted my life as I knew it to come to an end.

When I left the hospital, I began to put my life back together. I found a small job in a coffee shop after simplifying my skills on my CV. I got a really small apartment near the train station. It wasn't a great place and at times didn't feel like the safest either, but it was a start. I came back a few months later for a check-up with my doctor, I saw an advertisement for a health assistant post. It didn't require any specific training but a lot of skills that I possessed. I applied and I got the job. I've been working there now for five years – helping many people like myself.

I've spent my whole life sacrificing so that one day I could feel secure. What I should have been doing was building memories and focusing on myself. My mental health is a battle I fight every day but when I work now, I feel like I've achieved something at the end of the day. I don't worry so much about the amount of money I earn but what places I can visit. I'm building my experiences.

I've spent my whole life sacrificing so that one day I could feel secure when there are no guarantees in life. You've just got to go out there and live the best life you can with the time you have left.

Kindness Through My Little Mirror
Karachi, Pakistan

Urwa's Story

When I had my daughter, I was relieved that the hard labour was over. It was twelve painful hours, but she was born healthy with no complications. I thought that would be the hardest part but then I had to raise her. My husband and I had shared a lot of values. We wanted her to have a sense of religion, humanity, and confidence. We wanted her to know that just because she was a girl, she didn't have to hold back her light to let the other boys shine. She could shine just as bright.

The most important lesson we learnt was when we were stuck in traffic one day. An elderly man came up to the car in front of us and was begging for money. The man in the car in front spat in his face. My husband was alarmed. The elderly man had a walking stick, looked dirty, hungry and just broken. My husband and I looked at one another and just knew what the other was thinking. My husband pulled the car to the side. I waited with my daughter who was now three. We decided to get the man a meal from one of the restaurants near us and some spare food for his journey. When we gave him the food, he cried and told us his story. The death of his wife caused him to lose everything. He had been hungry for days and now he felt like a prince. He wanted to repay us, but we insisted that the smile he had given us was payment enough.

I taught my daughter that she could have all the qualities she wanted but without kindness they meant nothing. Being kind is the most important thing we could ask for. We live in the city and her father works for a big company, but I don't want her to be comfortable. We have worked very hard and want her to know that.

On her sixth birthday, we invited her two best friends over and they both brought her a present. One of the presents was big, and the other was small. The friend who'd brought the big present was laughing at the smaller present. It was so hard for me to not intervene as I could see her other friend's face drop with sadness. I was so used to telling my daughter how to act and what to say but I decided that this time I'd sit back. It was not my place to raise another woman's child. I had to trust my daughter. So, I sat back and waited to see how she would respond.

She opened both presents with such excitement. She opened the big one first and said, "thank you." When she opened the smaller one, she jumped up and hugged her friend. "I like both my presents the same," she said. I remember feeling so proud because I knew that what I'd been teaching her was working.

A Mother's Purse

Antwerp, Belgium

Katherine's Story

It's hard being a parent. I want to give my child everything they want. I want to give them the world if I can. As a parent, I want them to know that they can depend on me for anything materialistic or emotional. I'm always there but that's not always easy to see.

For many years, we have been living paycheck to paycheck. The economy isn't too great. My husband is also hard to work with. When he doesn't like something, he will argue and get fired or quit. I have tried a few times to also work as we need the money but every time I went to find something he would say I was a bad mother for leaving my child. I left it because I often felt it was true.

Since my son was young, I've tried to show him that we can't always afford the things that we want. I wanted him to learn to save so that when he wants something he can get it for himself. It saddens me if I think about it too much but there's not been a lot that I can do. I can talk to my husband as much as I want, but he has his own brain and doesn't want to listen.

When my purse is full, I show my son. When my purse is empty, I show my son. I show him everything so he doesn't think I'm hiding anything from him. I don't want him to think that I'm just being mean when I say no. I want him to know that when we have money, we have to prioritise our rent, bills and food. I'm trying to teach him to live within his means.

Things have been especially hard lately. My husband has missed a few paycheques.

My son is going back to school, and we couldn't get new supplies for this year. I knew he wanted them but when I showed my son my purse, he told me, "Don't worry, Mum, we'll get them when the wallet is full."

The other day, I went with him to get the food supplies for the month. He saw that I was upset because we couldn't get all the things we needed. I kept putting things back that we could go without. When we got home, my son ran off to his room and brought me his own savings. He said to me, "Don't worry, Mum, now your purse can be full again."

I've been looking for a job ever since. I don't have much experience but now that he is older, I'm hoping to do some office work in a school. I don't want him to suffer because his father isn't reliable. I don't want him thinking I'm a bad mother. That's why I want to work. I want him to know I did everything I could despite my circumstances. I did it to help him. My son has big dreams to fly aeroplanes. I want to help him achieve them.

Anxiety and Me
Bogotá, Colombia

Celia's Story

I was the best student in my high school.

I was always at the top of the list when I got my exam results. I put so much pressure on myself to do well that I never failed a class. I would spend hours reading my textbooks. I read everything – even the things not on our syllabus. I always wanted to be prepared and ready.

Unfortunately, I got really ill during the tenth grade, and I quickly started to fall behind. I felt like every minute I was not in the classroom; I was missing out on so much learning. That's when the panic attacks began. I didn't want to fail but I also knew my health would not be able to improve if I continued to stress. Knowing this made everything worse. I was away from school for six months before I came back. One day the teacher handed me an envelope with my report card that had all my grades on it, and I couldn't breathe. My heart was beating so fast. I felt detached. I hadn't even opened the envelope and I remember I felt like I wanted to die. I saw people trying to talk to me, but I couldn't hear them. My teacher kept telling me to calm down. "It's okay to not have done the best but remember you did well for someone who missed so much." I didn't even care. I just kept thinking I could have done better. I should have done better. Eventually, I passed out and woke up in the hospital.

The attacks were almost daily after that.

Last year I started college and I couldn't be the best student there no matter how hard I tried. Everyone was so talented. I felt like I just couldn't keep up with them. My panic attacks went from bad to worse – to the point I had to cancel my first semester. After I returned to college, I decided to start working on acknowledging my anxiety and not letting it hold me back anymore.

I used to try to hide it.

Everything I saw triggered me. Everyone seemed to be living this great life and fulfilling their passions whilst I was stuck. I would log off social media when I saw these amazing things my friends and family were achieving. I wouldn't answer calls because people would bombard me with questions about what I was doing and where I was going. I didn't have the answer. I thought that if nobody knew that the problem wouldn't exist. The more I tried to hide it though, the harder it became to cope. I've learned that the more I talk about my problem, the more I realise that other people experience similar things. People are more understanding than I thought they would be. I'm still trying to express it more – I'm just learning how best to do that.

One of the best pieces of advice I got whilst I was at college was from a great teacher I had. She told me, "Instead of letting anxiety keep you from doing your art, let it be the thing that motivates your art."

Once I stepped back and started to talk about my anxiety, I saw it reflected in my art pieces. Now that I didn't feel like I needed to perform at the top of my game every time, my art was freer. More expressive. I didn't have such stiff lines and forced imagery but rather open shapes which better captured the feeling of my paintings.

My anxiety is still a battle I face every day but I'm learning to do better with it. I'm learning that I don't have to be the best all the time, I just have to be me.

Sacrificing Today for a Better Someday
Brooklyn, New York, USA

Roxanne's Story

My mum left the Philippines when I was five years old.

I don't remember it that well. The day she left. I remember my dad telling me, that it was important that she went. She was doing it for our family. My sister and I were very young at the time. My dad was always there for us, but he become disconnected very quickly. He became a statue in our lives. He didn't talk very much and something in him just didn't seem to work. He woke us up in the morning, went to work, came home and went to bed. When we spoke to him, his eyes were always hollow. I think my mum leaving left a large void in his life. I'd like to think they were best friends. When my mum was here, the two of them were inseparable. They were always laughing. Always talking. I think not being able to talk every day caused a strain on my dad and their relationship. My sister and I basically raised each other because my dad became just a passenger in our lives.

As hard as it was for us at home, I think it must have been harder on my mother. Her visa status didn't let her come back home – even to just visit, and we didn't have the money to go see her. International phone calls cost a lot back then, so we managed to talk to her on the phone about once a month, but the line would often get cut as we ran out of credit. Mum would send us letters, clothes, and toys. We could tell those gifts and letters were sent out of guilt. She missed all our birthdays, school holidays and festive events. She missed us deeply. We all had one another in the Philippines. Dad may not have been there emotionally, but he knew he still had his girls to come home to at the end of the day. My mum had no support from her family or friends. She was alone and we were ungrateful. At that age we didn't care what went on behind the scenes, we just went with the fact. We didn't care what her reason was, my mum wasn't there for us. That's all we cared about – the rest was just excuses to us.

It took ten years of working and saving for her to finally bring us over. My mum had worked two jobs and studied. She wanted to do the best she could for us and knew that started with her being the best she could be for herself. My mum definitely struggled but most of that was behind closed doors, and we never really understood it.

The reunion was different from what she had imagined in her head. Well, I think it was anyways. She probably expected us to be overjoyed with seeing her and grateful for the sacrifices she made for her family, but it wasn't like that. My sister and I were teenagers by then. We had spent ten years in difficulty. My father had completely zoned out on us. By the age of ten, we were having to pick up after him. He became depressed and we felt we weren't enough for him. We saw that with each parcel we received from my mum, it just made him worse. We saw that side of it, and we resented her for it. We resented her for leaving us to look after ourselves. We resented her for not being able to visit – although we knew deep down it wasn't because she didn't want us. We resented her for missing so much of our lives – the important years. The biggest disappointment for her though, I think, was that we ignored her when we were finally a whole family. We weren't used to being told what to do. My sister and I had practically done everything ourselves – with some help from the elderly lady that lived in the apartment below ours in the Philippines.

We were pretty awful to my mum in the first few years of our lives in America.

My father divorced my mum soon after we arrived. He was tired of feeling like a second choice to her. My sister and I struggled at school and took that out on my mum. We were bullied for our lack of English and once we grasped the English language, we were mocked for our accents or the way we looked. Everyone kept saying, "Go back home you Chinks." We were too startled by the comment to even correct them. We hated our mum for bringing us here when we were just bullied at school. We hated her because our father left us. We just hated her.

But her sacrifice paid off.

My mum worked day and night around us to send both my sister and me to college. Even when we shouted and screamed at her, Mum would always have dinner ready and on the table by seven o'clock and our lunches packed for school in the morning. She wouldn't always be there in the morning because of her job but the table was set for breakfast. When we were at college, she left us more money for transport. She didn't want us to work, so she worked herself into the ground to support us. My mum wanted nothing to stop us from showing that she didn't sacrifice our childhood in vain. We both graduated college at the top of our classes and have really good jobs now.

It wasn't until I started working that I realised how hard and lonely it really was for my mum. My sister and I both started to realise how horrible we had been to her. My mum sacrificed everything for us.

We now had the opportunity to earn more, have a better family life and have a better education than we ever would have had in the Philippines. The things that made us different in school – the things we were picked on for, made us stand out for all the right reasons. You can't even tell that I only came to New York ten years ago now.

My mum still works but she's cut back on her hours significantly. My sister and I brought my mum her first house. It's in this neighbourhood that she'd always wanted us all to live in when we first moved here but she said, "I don't think I'll ever be able to afford to live here. Among nature and the chitter-chatter of children." My mum cried with happiness when we gave her the keys and the paperwork with her name on it. It's only a five-minute walk from my sister's apartment and across the street from where I live. We both insisted we could pay for her to live comfortably but she wanted to work. It was all she had left now. The three of us are really close now. We realised the error of our ways.

We haven't seen my father since he divorced my mum. I think that's what made me love my mum more. In the ten years that she was away, she still tried to contact us. She worked her ass off to reunite us and when we got here, she did not stop. She took care of all of us – even when we treated her like a punching bag. In the ten years that we have been in New York, my mum has looked after us better than in the ten years we lived with my dad. Even through all the pain we have caused her.

My sister and I don't think we'll ever be able to make up for our initial behaviour towards our mum, but we try to every day. Sometimes we stay at her house and sometimes we just have tea, but we make sure we check in with her. We are constantly trying to make up for the lost time.

It was only once I was an adult, I truly understood how lonely those ten years must have been for her and how wrong we were to have taken them for granted.

Surviving Sunday
Cairo, Egypt

Nadia's Story

I was married when I was seventeen. It wasn't weird or wrong like many young people perceive it now. It was normal and I wanted to. It was arranged but I met my now-husband a few times after my family said yes.

What made me say yes? He asked at our first meeting if I actually wanted to get married. He wanted me to be sure a life-long commitment was what I wanted now or if I wanted to wait a little longer. He said that he was in but just because my parents had said yes, didn't mean I had to agree. I'd never been asked for my opinion before, my father just agreed or disagreed, and I followed. That's how I was raised. I met him twice more, but I knew after ten minutes of talking to him that I wanted to say yes.

My whole life became about my family.

Together we had four beautiful children. My life was simple. I barely had to leave our house because my husband brought me everything I needed or wanted. I was happy. I was far too innocent though – I regret that now. I asked my husband about his day and how work was going but I had no interest in learning more about what his job actually involved. I was happy sticking to my work in the house.

I had no idea about anything, but the world has a way of teaching you.

Fifteen years ago, my husband died suddenly. I was making tea one Sunday afternoon and I called him a few times wondering if he wanted to have anything to eat. I kept calling him, but he wouldn't respond and that's when I found out. By that Sunday evening, I was suddenly having to become the head of the family. I needed to support my children who were still young. I put together a list of what my husband did. The shopping he did on a Friday, the business he went to from Monday to Saturday and the two hours he spent in the evening helping the children with their homework.

My husband owned an upholstery shop. I had no idea what they did there. I just knew how to sew – nothing about woods or machinery. I went to the shop in my best black clothes with a notebook and pen. My husband built this company from nothing to a well-earning shop. I had no qualifications to do anything else, so I went to learn about the business and support my children.

When I arrived there, the men in the shop sympathised with my loss. When they asked how they could help, I told them, "I need to learn the business. I will now be your boss." They acted like they were doing me a favour. The workers tried to convince me to let them handle the business, but I couldn't trust them. Every time I went to see what they were doing; they couldn't get rid of me fast enough. I went in one Sunday because I knew no one would have been there and used my husband's keys to get in. I went through the finance books. I didn't know much about math, but I knew addition and subtraction. I could do the basics and I did. I learnt they were hiding the profits from me.

I had to take over. There was no other choice. My kids were still in school, and that money belonged to them.

I began going to the shop every day. It wasn't well-received by the workers. At first, they tried to box me out of everything. I'm pretty sure they thought they could push me out. They knew I didn't understand the business so they wouldn't explain anything. They made every job more difficult by giving me more information than I needed or no information at all. They hid the numbers from me. When a client entered the store, they wouldn't even introduce me as the owner but tried to hide me from people.

I didn't give up though. I sat there and watched every move they made. I memorised everything. On Sundays when the shop was closed, I brought my children with me and whilst they sat in the office and finished off their homework, I learnt how the machinery worked. I learnt how costing was done. I learnt who our supplier was. I put in the time to learn every fine string of my husband's business.

After forty days, there were some new rules at the shop. The workers were not allowed to speak to the client directly. Anyone who went behind my back was given their notice. All orders had to be written and signed off by me. The change was hard, but it's got a lot better.

This shop is my children's and I'm its caretaker until they're ready to take over.

A Home of My Own
Tengah, Singapore

Sophea's Story

I grew up moving from place to place. We had houses but never any real home. Most children my age wanted to be doctors or economists when they were older. All I dreamed of was owning my own home. I never wanted something big. It didn't matter to me the size. I just wanted four walls that I could call my own.

I was forty-five years old, and I was tired of renting a room. I always felt like it was too much pressure. Each month passed by so quickly and the landlord would be knocking on my door asking for his money. If I didn't have the money, he would knock every day. I couldn't take the stress.

I just wanted a place where I could relax.

It was a long process and very tiring. I picked up extra shifts and put my money into committees so that I could save. At many points, I thought I wouldn't be able to afford anything. The house prices kept increasing but my wage stayed the same. I was determined though. I had wanted this for so long that I refused to give it up. I had given a lot up in my life – love, the chance to have children, and going to college, but I wasn't willing to sacrifice this.

After two long years, I saved enough money to buy a house in the slum. It wasn't a legal house because it was built on government land, but it was all I could afford. It wasn't the most visually appealing house, but I didn't mind. It was mine. I tried to make it nicer. On my walk home from work every day, I gathered scrap wood. I'd always been good with my hands so I used the wood to create an extra room. I even built my own bathroom. I slept so well there. Nothing was troubling me, and I never had to worry about someone knocking on my door for money.

One day though I came home to find a letter stuck on my door. Everyone in our slum got the same red letter. Eviction. It said we needed to leave because the government was planning to build a road on the land. I had lived here for seven years and now had to give up this paradise I had created for myself. I went out that afternoon to see what I could do. I had a substantial amount of savings but that would not be enough to buy a home in the current housing climate. I panicked but I knew I'd find somewhere to rent. It wasn't ideal but it was a start.

Armed guards came the next morning and bulldozed all our houses. They didn't even check if everyone had been evacuated, they just wanted to get the job done. That was three years ago. They still haven't built the road, but they inconvenienced over two hundred families.

I still haven't managed to move into my own home but I'm getting a lot closer. I've managed to change jobs to one that pays me significantly more and am looking to find a place. I think I can afford to live in a better neighbourhood this time, but I'll have to wait until next month to see. The good news though, is that I'm not as stressed now about having to pay my rent. I have my money every month ready for him. I know I'm a lot luckier than many other people but there's still a different comfort to having a place to call your own.

I'm not giving up on that dream just yet.

My Unicorn Uterus
Mexico City, Mexico

Selena's Story

I'd had five operations on my uterus by the time I was twenty-three. I had consistent cyst growth and each time they grew, they kept damaging my lining. For the past four years, I had spent days of my life holed up in my bedroom – unable to move, unable to sleep and unable to do almost anything because the pain had gotten so bad. My life felt like it was put on hold as I didn't have the energy to study at college or socialise with friends. After each surgery, I felt like I was going to die from the pain. I wasn't sure how many more surgeries I was going to last. I wasn't even sure if I would have a life worth living after all of this.

One night I found myself finally able to enjoy a night out with my friends. It was the first time in a long while that I wasn't worried about what time to take my medicine or when my next hospital appointment was. I was simply having fun being a reckless student. I met a handsome boy that night. He was smart. He knew the right words to say and when to say them. We hung out a few times after that night and it was on our fourth or fifth date that I thought I would tell him about my health. I explained it to him as best I could but the entire time I spoke, he looked at me like I was hollow. I think he decided then that I was too much to deal with.

He walked out the door that day and I didn't see or hear from him for weeks.

Sitting in the consulting room with my doctor once more, I sunk into my seat as the doctor went through all my options. After my last surgery, the scan results suggested that juristic action needed to be taken. My doctor explained it to me at great length and by the end of our session, he was scheduling surgery to have my uterus completely removed. My heart sunk. I wanted to have a baby so much. I thought after all this it would be something I could have for myself. A consolation for the pain. It almost felt like hearing my life as I knew it was over.

A week later, I started feeling strange. Stranger than I had ever felt before. My back pain was still there but nausea became a more permeant fixture of my mornings. I craved bread all the time and I fell asleep anywhere at any time. I always had problems with my hormone levels, so I thought it was nothing – just my body psyching itself out for the surgery in a few weeks. My friends would joke that I was pregnant when they came to visit once but it was a painful arrow to my heart even when they joked. I knew for me that this would not be a possibility.

Three days before my surgery, the aches and pains in my body became so bad that I had to spend the entire day in bed. My head was spinning and every time I tried to get up, I felt like I was going to blackout. When my friend came over that evening, I kept falling everywhere – I could barely sit up straight. She forced me to go to the hospital and had my neighbour help her carry me out of the house and into her car.

In the hospital, they ran every test they could, but I don't remember any of that. What I do remember is my doctor coming into the room to postpone my surgery indefinitely. He said, "Unless you would insist, we do not feel comfortable removing a uterus when there is a seven-week-old foetus in there." I blinked like I had just been hit by headlights.

Pulling myself out of my bed, I went to the hospital pharmacy and brought ten pregnancy tests. When I finished using them, I put them down thinking I was crazy. I didn't want to be let down again. Then, right before I was about to leave the hospital, I checked each one. As each stick showed a positive sign, my smile grew larger and larger with tears running down my face. After all that stress and worry, it was going to happen.

I still have those tests somewhere in my house today. I also have a beautiful daughter. Whenever I look at her, I think about how they were going to remove my uterus only three days later. I've been fortunate with my daughter all these years. I've had my uterus removed now but that pain I had before her, feels like small pinches compared to the joy she has brought me.

Rejection
Larkana, Pakistan

Rashida's Story

I knew from a very young age that I was different. I never felt comfortable in my body and there were times I would find myself dancing around the clothes on the washing line – dreaming of myself in every woman's suit that hung there.

My family realised very early on what was happening. I was the youngest of five children (two boys, two girls) and they saw that I thought differently. That I looked like their boys but acted like their girls. They tried to get me to watch cricket and get involved in wrestling or kite running but I wasn't interested in those things. I was interested in my studies and fashion. I did enjoy playing cricket with my family but that had nothing to do with my gender and more to do with my happiness. I was always happiest when I was just myself with my family.

Transgender kids in our city are usually sent off to live with other transgender people. We are not provided with the opportunity to make something of ourselves. We are forced to make a living by dancing or singing because there are no other options. Nothing else besides selling our bodies for sex but that's not what we want. My family tried to send me to live with a group of transgender people who lived just outside our city, but I ran away before they could. I ran away to our local Maulana who lived just down the road. I explained to him my predicament and he did not judge me –he understood. He understood that it had nothing to do with the way I was raised. He understood that the problem with my parents accepting me had nothing to do with my religion. My religion recognised that transgender people are accepted and that there was nothing wrong with it. The problem was rather with my culture. My society. My family weren't ready to accept the consequences of my decisions. Of my feelings. The

Maulana explained the situation to my family and after much discussion, it was agreed that I could stay at home with my family.

When I first came home, it was very awkward. My family had accepted me being in the house, but they still did not accept me. It was one evening when my mother came into my bedroom. She sat down next to me on my bed, and she said, "beta, I cannot make everyone accept your decision. We all have our own views and opinions. We have to think about how we are going to deal with the consequences of your decision. We have to think about our family honour and although you are doing nothing wrong, people in our society are not so understanding and will see this as a dishonour to our family. I have spoken to your father, and we want you to have the best possible opportunity. We would like, with your agreement, for you to finish your education to whatever level you like before making any final decisions. You can be whatever you like but without education how can you help any community."

Once word got out about my transition, life became a lot harder. I went to school, but I had to dress like a boy. I was not allowed to sit anywhere near girls and the boys spent a lot of time taunting me. My teachers in particular made life difficult. I was given a lot more work than most boys in my class with a much shorter deadline. My teachers made me sing and dance to entertain my class. Sometimes, I would be held back a whole year because I would refuse. I learnt very quickly that no matter where I went or how much money my parents were willing to throw at the problem, I would now have to play society's game.

As I grew up and became more confident with my gender, people began to advise me more. They kept telling me that I needed to get some skills and start working better jobs, but little did these people know, that I had a double master's degree. I thought (my parents prayed) that having an education would solve a lot of the problems that came with being transgender, but it solved nothing. I still had to beg, and I still had to dance. I moved to Karachi where there was a bigger transgender community, hoping there would be greater opportunities but for years there was nothing. I got so low that for a whole year I prayed. I thought, if fate were in my own hands, I'd be happy to be a dog just so I could live with my own mother. However, as I saw more and more women like me struggling, I knew that my mum and dad spent so much on my education so I could help them and myself.

After a lot of hard work and with the help of a local Maulana, I landed a job as a tax recovery officer, and I worked there for four years. At times I faced a lot of verbal abuse, but my co-workers were supportive. I had my own office so I could cut myself off from the world when things got too much but I really loved my job there. After four years, I was in a meeting with the welfare minister when she offered me a job. She wanted me to run a Transgender community centre that was being initiated by the government. I happily took the job, but it wasn't what I had dreamt of. After a year, the funds from the government began to drop and my pay was almost just two percent of our original agreement. The centre that was supposed to be a safe environment for transgender people became a target for yobs. We had women being raped on their way or shot at outside the building. The police often turned a blind eye.

It has been really hard to get our voices heard but after a lot of campaigning, we are beginning to see a change.

I am now working as a legal supporter for the community. I spend a lot of my time helping women get their identity cards from the NADRA office. There's a lot of abuse at the office from the workers and the visitors. We're working to get a separate window for us at the office so we can cut down on the abuse. I'm still working with the welfare minister to try and change the opportunities for transgender people.

A lot of people assume that transgender people are automatically sex workers but what they don't realise is, that if we were, our lives would actually be a lot better. We wouldn't have to beg or dance. We would just have to feel hollow all the time.

A Woman's Acumen
Jakarta, Indonesia

Mony's Story

I've been helping out here for the last year. I do as much as I can but I'm still learning the ropes. This is my older sister's business.

For most of my life, I've barely known my sister. I just knew her name and what the features on her face looked like from the pictures in our kitchen. We come from a small village south of Indonesia. My sister was the eldest girl. We had no brothers, and my father could not carry the burden of raising us all by himself. My sister moved to the city when I was a baby. Shortly after she moved, my father lost his job and she started supporting our whole family.

Everyone depended on her.

My sister sent us money every month, but I barely knew her. I was trapped in my own cycle of life – a life she was paying for. I went to school and then came home to help with the housework. I only spoke to her on the phone and even then, I didn't know what to say. I hadn't seen her since I was a baby, and I knew nothing about her besides what was told to me. I didn't know what she was interested in talking about or if she was even interested in talking to me. She was awfully polite, but it was awkward. All I could say to her was thank you but at times even that felt like too little.

A few years ago, after I finished my education, I followed in her footsteps and moved to Jakarta. I didn't think it was right for her to continue to carry the burden of our whole family on her back anymore. Especially when I was perfectly able to help. Now we've become very close.

I can finally witness the sacrifices that she's made for us.

She works all the time. She works tremendously hard. People keep thinking that you need an education to get somewhere but my sister has taken the skills she has and monopolised them. She owns a small restaurant and runs a furniture business out of her home. Both businesses are doing extremely well. Even though she's a woman, she does all the marketing and negotiating herself. A lot of the time, the men try to take advantage of her. They think that because she's a woman, she doesn't have an acumen for business. My sister surprises them every time they come by using more professional words – ones she'd learnt in the books she's studied from the library.

My sister wakes up early every morning to search for wood in old and broken buildings. She upcycles a lot, so her business costs stay relatively low. After her morning shift working on her furniture business, she comes to check on me at the restaurant. Before she leaves every day, she checks the accounts of both her businesses. When she comes home at night, her body is so tired that she goes directly to sleep. I always feel my heart break for her.

I want to become like her so she can rest but I'm afraid I'm too naive. My sister can manage all her jobs and knows how to handle even the most difficult situations. I want to take over for her but right now I'm still learning. I don't want to ruin what she's worked so hard to build.

My sister has spent her entire life sacrificing for all of us, and I want her to be able to make decisions for herself now. I know she wants to travel the world, so I've started putting aside some of my pay for her. When it's grown a bit more, I'm going to give it to her – hopefully by then she'll know she can trust me with her business.

When I watch her, I feel like she can do anything.

From Success to Significance
Gainesville, Florida, USA

Jane's Story

I've lived in Florida almost all my life. I grew up there. Had my first kiss outside the cinema. Met the love of my life in high school. Had my first heartbreak at the milkshake shack with the love of my life. Florida was everything to me. It was my home.

I started my career as a teller at a community bank in Florida. I wasn't too old then – maybe in my early thirties, but the job was fine for me and it paid my rent. I had a young child at that time, so I just wanted to be able to support them.

As time went on, I kept moving up. I wouldn't say I'm overly ambitious and the money didn't drive me (although it did help). I just have a lot of motivation. I quickly became tired and wanted to do more. I wanted to know what was next and where this was going. I'd always ask the next question or apply for the next job. I needed something to feed my energy. So, I worked my way up to CEO. It was demanding but I enjoyed the position. It fulfilled my need for more.

Getting the balance between work and home life became a little tricky but I managed it. My family were everything to me and they supported me through and through. I was handling everything quite well until a few years ago when my husband passed away. Then my mother. Then my best friend. All in a single year.

One after the other.

I'd never even lived alone before. I went from my parents to my husband's. Suddenly I felt unanchored. I was lost with all these questions and reached this place of not knowing. I just kept asking myself *what do I do now?* I couldn't go back to making more money. It didn't mean anything to me if I couldn't spend it on the people I loved. I wasn't driven by that.

So, I decided to make a change.

I went back to college to get a master's in public administration. I'm just waiting for my final class before I graduate. I've already got a job waiting – working with homeless people. We're working toward getting homeless people into permanent housing and I'm really excited. I want to be in a place where I can change some lives. A place where I can mean something to someone-I can mean something to myself. It feels like I've moved from success to significance.

The Animal Whisperer
Anzali, Iran

Zaynab's Story

My daughter has a heart for animals.

When she was little, she spent a lot of time with her grandparents. My husband and I both worked so they would look after her whenever they could. My parents had lots of birds. Budgies, parrots, and canaries. My father fed them every morning before breakfast and when my daughter was with them, she too would feed the birds.

On her daily walks with her grandfather, my daughter saw lots of stray cats and dogs walking. She particularly liked the small cats. She carried a rucksack with her wherever she went. On her daily walks, if she saw a small kitten, she would put them in her bag and leave the zip halfway open. When she got back to her grandparents' house, she would run to the kitchen and fill a bowl with milk. She would then open her rucksack to reveal a litter of kittens – all drinking milk on the marble floor of my parents' house.

Over the years, she has left bowls of water and some left-over food outside both our home and her grandparents' house. She wanted to make sure that the stray animals had something when she wasn't there to help them.

My daughter is about to start applying for university. She has worked really hard to achieve the best grades for veterinary school. Our closest university for a veterinary degree is in Tehran. There aren't many universities that teach people to care for animals. My daughter wants to start her own charity to help dogs and cats.

I worry that she will get her heart broken. In Iran, we have no culture for animals. We like them for a short time, but we have more cats and dogs on the street than we do in our houses. Animal lovers are seen as a little strange.

I try to encourage her. That is my job as a mother. Whenever she talks about it, I see her eyes light up. Whenever she sees an animal, she immediately approaches it and gives it some water from her bag. She always carries spare water bottles just in case. Animals make her happy. She knows better than to ask to take any stray home. Her father wouldn't let them stay but she is happy to just see them well.

Secretly, I don't want her to do it.

Last year she saw a cat break its leg on the street. Without telling me, she took a taxi all the way to Tehran, just to find a veterinarian. People in my community made comments when they heard but she did not care. She thinks she may have saved the cat's life.

She is still very much shielded from the difficulties of loving animals in Iran. She is determined not to give up. She thinks she can change people's minds and be a compass for compassion. She's packing for university at the moment. She's going to be a vet.

I will support her no matter what. I just hope life will be kinder to her than people can be towards animals.

Self-Conservation Living Among Conservatives
Rajput, India

Alia's Story

I belong to a very conservative family, so I have to deal with a lot of permission issues.

There are a lot of boundaries for me. It's frustrating because I just want to go out there and explore my options. I haven't even seen that much beyond my house and my school in my own city. I want to be more independent. A lot of my friends are allowed to go out to restaurants together for food after school or can decide last minute to go for ice cream or to the cinema. I have to ask for everything and even if I am allowed to go, I'm never allowed to go unchaperoned. I'm driven there, my friends are checked, and their parent's numbers are exchanged with mine and then I'm picked up later.

I see so much potential in myself when I look in the mirror. I often wonder if my family even bother to look at me and see just how much I can do.

Most of the women in my family are housewives and my father would prefer me to become a housewife as well. We live in a joint family system, so I get a lot of pressure from my uncles and grandfather to focus less on school and more on my house skills. My aunties and my mum will try and help me where they can. Sometimes they take on my workload so I can study for my tests or do some extra revision, but my grandmother scolds them. Ultimately, my grandmother doesn't believe any woman will ever break the barrier and be able to achieve their 'working' goal, so she'd rather I learn that the hard way now rather than later.

I refuse to bow down to it though.

I've been working so hard in school. I'm studying all the time – any moment I can. These exams are so tough, but I don't want all this hard work to be wasted.

I put in so much effort so that I can prove that my house is not my limit. My grades will prove that I have more potential than they believe me to be capable of. I want to be a businesswoman. I want to employ other women so they too can see they don't just have to be a housewife. There's nothing wrong with being a housewife but there is often much more a girl desires than being told she just needs to cook, clean and look after the family all day when she is older. I want to give women the opportunity to be more. To have options.

My mother is a housewife. She needs to ask my father for everything. When he's not around, she tells me, "Do exactly what you want to do."

My mum is my biggest supporter and when I passed my exams, she was the first person to congratulate me. She knows I'm going to be able to do anything I set my mind to.

Just When I Thought I Failed
Istanbul, Turkey

Leena's Story

We've never had a lot of money. Both my husband and I work but we've had a lot of medical bills. I had my last child early and needed to put him in a NIC Unit. I needed a lot of blood transfusions and surgery to fix a rupture in my uterus. We lost him after three months, but the bills never went away.

After a tiring day at work, my three-year-old daughter came up to me and asked me how everything had been. She was little but had a big imagination. I took some worthless coins out of my pocket and jokingly told her that she was now a very rich little girl and she needed to protect these. She waited to show them to her father at dinner that evening and then hid them away. I had forgotten about them. Around the same time, my oldest daughter was celebrating her birthday and received a substantial amount of money from her aunts and uncles. She too put it away safely.

A few months later, we were drowning in overdue bills. The hospital bills would not go down, but neither would rent nor electricity or water. My husband and I were doing the best we possibly could and although we scraped together enough to pay our bills for the month, we did not have enough for food. We felt like our pride was in our stomachs as we approached my oldest daughter. We felt ashamed even thinking about it, but we had no other option. We asked her, "Could we please use some of your birthday money for groceries. We'll give it back to you as soon as we can but right now, we're in a really tight position." She refused.

My husband went to hide in our room whilst I sat on our sofa. I started to think about what we could sell to hold us over. I had already sold as much of my jewellery as I could and sold a lot of our household appliances. I thought about my oldest daughter, and I almost started crying. I began to think that I had completely failed as a parent. Suddenly I felt a tug on my shoulder and saw my youngest beside me. She began to whip my face with one of her hands and then told me to cover my eyes. She had such a big smile on her face that I did exactly as she told me. I felt her pulling on my hand and I could feel something cold on my palm. Opening my eyes, I could see my youngest daughter's bright smile as she gave me back the handful of coins I had given her.

"Now you're rich, Mummy, so you don't have to worry," she said to me.

I went to bed that day with such pride. It may have not fixed the woes in my head, but my youngest daughter fixed the woe in my heart.

Hope
Leeds, England

Farzana's Story

I was born with a club foot. It's a minor thing but where we're from, it brings a big stigma with it. My brain did not matter and no matter how hard I tried with my education and no matter how well I did, my club foot reminded people that there was a problem with me.

My marriage happened when I was twenty years old. My husband was ten years older than me, but I did not mind. We both got on really well and the relationship between our families was strong. Life with my in-laws was really good. They lived well and their business meant that they could afford to provide me with a good life, but my husband understood that even though they had money, it was not everything. My in-laws lived in a village and although we owned the factory there, there was little scope to go further. To have more. My husband and I discussed it and decided that I would apply for a visa to England. He said this could be my opportunity to study and once he had made arrangements for his parents, he too would come over. It took a while for me to get my visa but my sister, who already lived in England, helped me through the process. The day after my visa came, I was on the next flight to England.

Life in England was a lot harder than I think anyone anticipated. A month after I arrived, I found out I was pregnant. My sister's husband (who also happened to be my cousin), was already unhappy with having me but the idea of having a baby in the house seemed to make him more unhappy. I really wanted to go back and just be with my family, but my husband told me I'd have to make the sacrifice. That I needed to stay for the family and that he would be over as soon as he could. I studied and worked. I contributed to the house as much as I could whether it was financially or physically. I had a little girl, and I tried my best to not step on anyone's toes but as the years passed, things only got harder.

I had to continue listening to my sister's husband make constant comments about my daughter and me. I had to learn to hide away and often found myself spending more and more time out of the house, whether it be spending longer at work or taking a little bit longer to do the shopping.

My sister has been a real rock for me though. I don't think I would have done as much as I have without her – I don't think I would have stayed here without her. My sister helped me raise my daughter, including her alongside her own two children, who were a few years older. She helped with looking after her when I had my exams or work. As time passed, our kids went to the same school, so she helped me with drop-offs in the morning when I had early shifts.

I still longed for my husband, but his circumstances became more difficult. He was one of three boys and whilst his brothers had come over to England years before we were even married, the plan was always for all of them to move here. Their family plan was for one to set up the business and then for another to come over and then another. However, their father's health seriously deteriorated after their mother passed away in the first year of my marriage. My husband didn't want to leave him, and his father didn't want to leave his lifelong home. So, we had to make sacrifices. Every time we tried to get my husband to come over and one of his brothers to take care of their father for a short while, they declined. My husband comes over for a couple of months a year and I try and go back for a month but it's hard because we have such a limited time together.

My father-in-law died a year ago now so I finally thought my family could be reunited after eight years. My husband spoke to his brothers, and they said they would help with his application. I had to start earning more so that he could come over and they said they would give me a job in their family business. I packed up my life here with my sister and my now seven-year-old daughter and we moved to Milton Keynes to finally get my husband over here.

However, his family made life difficult for me. They paid me the same amount I was earning at my old job but made me do double the work. The hours were inconvenient for my daughter – I wasn't there to drop her off or pick her up from school, and matters were made worse when they refused to help. Back in Leeds, I had my sister helping me with my daughter. I had friends and a great work environment. I had left a network of support behind for a much harder life in Milton Keynes, but I didn't give up – I couldn't. I had worked hard for eight years now, and this was finally a chance for my husband to come. I didn't want to lose him just because I was finding things hard. I stayed for one month in

Milton Keynes but eventually, my husband told me to go back. He heard about what was going on and decided we didn't need his family to make ours complete.

I was back in Leeds. It felt like square one all over again, but I kept smiling. I kept going because it was now or never to reunite my family. I spoke with my bosses at my old job, and they helped me more than I could have asked. They've increased my hours so that I can start earning more. I'm saving as much money as possible so that I can show that I can support a family.

It's been eight years, but it finally feels like it's going to happen. Like we're going to be a whole soon. I can feel it and that's what's keeping me going.

A Mother Without a Child
Lahore, Pakistan

Zara's Story

I couldn't have children. It made me depressed. My body failed in the one thing it was built to do. My husband was extremely supportive and told me God would give us a child. I just had to have faith.

One day on the way back from teaching at our local school, I saw a young girl curled up by a tree. She was no more than four. She couldn't speak. I remember looking around for her parents. She had bruises on her arms and a cut on her head. I took her to the police station. They said they couldn't do anything for her except put her in a children's home. I heard about those and couldn't bring myself to do that to her. I brought her home with me after telling the police to put out a found persons report so that her parents could find her safe and sound.

I've looked after her now for twelve years. My husband and I have almost finished processing her adoption papers and are just waiting for the final paperwork. We now wanted to make sure she knew we were permeant. In both her heart and in the eyes of the law.

She has had a difficult time. When she first came home, she was starving. I warmed up a plate of rice that was left in our fridge until I could make dinner and she ate it faster than anyone I have ever seen before. She was shy, especially toward my husband. She didn't let him come close to her for weeks. It was slow but she's now been falling asleep on his chest every night for the past seven years.

Our biggest change has come in her studies. She was illiterate when she first came home with me. She could not read, write or even speak properly. We communicated through pictures or by pointing at things. She did not understand a lot of what I was saying but we got through it – slowly. I never wanted to scare her off.

She is still very shy. She doesn't speak up for herself and lets people push her around. I noticed at school many times, that the girls would taunt her for her haircut or her shoes. They would push her around, but she would do nothing. Say nothing.

I'm afraid if someone harms her, she wouldn't tell me.

She has always kept her problems to herself. I still don't know what she was doing under a tree when I found her, and I don't want to know now. However, with the headlines as they are, I always tell her it's important for her to tell me if anyone touches her in any way that makes her uncomfortable or harms her. I don't learn about things that happen to her until they are reflected in her behaviour at home. Recently I found her washing the dishes, and I asked her where she learned to do that. She told me, "When I visit my friend's house, I do the dishes all the time."

It's still a slow process. We work every day to make sure she has the best chance. That she is the happiest she can be.

Last week after dinner, my husband turned to me after our daughter had gone to do her homework. He said to me, "I told you to have faith in God. God knew we did not need a blank page to be parents to, we just needed the right child."

I have never regretted my decision to pick her up that day and my husband couldn't have been any more supportive. He reminded me through all our tough times – through all my tears and miscarriages, that we'd have a child. His certainty always pained me more because the idea felt further and further away every time I used to think about it. He knew what I always should have.

We just needed to expand the way we thought.

Million Heart Painting
Tehran, Iran

Rahil's Story

When I was little, my ummi gave me a sketch pad and colours. Every day, whilst she worked, I would draw or colour whatever I wanted. We didn't have technology like we do now. I was an only child, and our TV didn't work all the time.

Over time, I spent all my spare time creating different art pieces. I wanted to create metaphoric pieces. Modern ideas through simple, relatable images. I made a lot of dark and twisted drawings, but I really liked them. I was proud of them.

Ummi and Abu didn't like how much time I spent on pictures. They saw all the doodles in my chemistry and biology books. They said I needed to focus on my studies now as my art would get me nowhere. I stopped creating for a couple of years. I resisted the urge to draw by picking up a book to read instead but my craving to draw was not satisfied. My parents did not recognise how hollow I became without my drawing. They were just happy with my schoolwork. I was still achieving the same good grades as I was when I was drawing but they didn't care about that. They were just glad I had stopped.

It was when I got into my first year of university that I started drawing small pieces during my lectures. They would often be on napkins or pieces of loose paper. I treasured them like they were gold – keeping them hidden between the pages of my textbooks. One day I was walking along the corridor and accidentally knocked into someone. A lecturer came to help me pick up the books that I had dropped. When he did, he noticed the drawings that had fallen out and asked me where they had come from. When he discovered they were mine, he insisted I stop whatever course I was doing and learn art. He said one day my drawings could be worth a lot of money. I dismissed the comments as they would not make my parents happy.

After making some phone calls, he came back to me a few days later. He had contacted a friend of his at a leading art university and they wanted to interview me. He said I needed to put a portfolio together so that I could show them my work. I didn't have anything besides the few drawings I had been drawing during my lectures that year. I told him there was no point. I was not prepared, and my parents would never pay for me to go there. They didn't want me to pursue my art. He told me to go to the interview anyway and the rest would be in the hands of God. I got offered a place as soon as my interview finished.

The kind professor called my parents. He told them being a scientist or doctor is a good profession but being these things did not make me happy. His conversation with my parents changed everything for me.

I've been going to art school for two years now on a full scholarship. My parents still don't get my dreams, but they'll support them – even if they're still very critical about it, they haven't tried to stop me. I can now finally admit it. I'm trying to be an artist.

My ummi is still more difficult to communicate with than my abu. She thinks all artists are just rebels who live their lives in sin. She doesn't understand that my art doesn't change who I am. It just lets me express my thoughts more creatively. Ummi thinks that my art will lead me nowhere, but I don't mind. I'm still trying to convince both of them that I made the right decision.

I showed a painting to my ummi. I was like, "Do you like it?"

And she was like, "I guess, but why is there a cigarette? Are you smoking now?"

And I was like, "No, ummi. The cigarette represents pain."

And she was like, "Did we not love you enough?"

I have my first art show next week. I'm hoping to take both of them and then they will see. They will then see what art means for the soul.

Dancing Through It All
Jerusalem, Israel

Audrey's Story

I was the youngest in the family.

The Nazis had already taken Austria and there were rumours they were beginning to invade boarding nations, so my family had made the decision to move. I went to Israel first and the rest of my family were supposed to join me shortly.

The war was extremely disruptive to everyone. Everyone's light went out and we were all on red alert all the time. In Poland, I was training to be a ballerina. I loved the discipline. The adrenaline from performing. My mum wanted me to go ahead to Israel first so that I could find a new ballet class. The fears of an invasion had caused many social activities to stop and unfortunately my ballet was a social activity. I had not trained for six months professionally before having to seek refuge but my mum insisted I continued. My whole family did. In Poland I was on my way to being admitted into an international ballet school; one of the best. My family said I had great potential and to not lose what made me so special, so happy. When I got to Israel, I could not care less about my ballet. I waited for my family.

Over two years, we sent letters back and forth between us. My older brothers had had to join the army. The youngest couldn't make the journey without my mother and father. The climate was becoming increasingly dangerous and any movement between borders could have been deadly. We all had to wait. We all tried to keep our spirits alive, my mum would tell me about the group of families that they would stay with and the performances the younger kids put on. I only did my ballet in my bedroom but told my family that I was in a class and had various productions. They were so proud, and I did not want to dampen their spirits especially as I heard about conditions worsening in Poland.

The last letter I got from Poland came in 1941 from my mother. She was asking me to save her some food.

Then the letters just stopped.

I knew Germany had occupied Poland and there were rumours about the things that were happening. I heard pieces and the family I was staying with left words lingering in the house, but I never learned any specifics. I don't think I wanted to know. I clung to the hope that they were just lost in the sea of madness.

As the war continued and my letters stopped, I finally joined a proper ballet class. I did not want my mother to be disappointed with how bad I had gotten in the time we had been apart. The ballet consumed all my time but more and more about the activities occurring in Europe began to become public knowledge.

When the war finished, I had been cast in the lead of our ballet production, but I couldn't do it. I began to see, hear and read about the horrors of the concentration camps and the Nazis that plagued them. I learnt of all the innocent people taken there. I learnt that they had been going on for years. All I could think about were my letters and my family. How they stopped. I still don't know for sure what happened to most of my family. I've been back to Poland many times to try and find out, but their deaths were not recorded on any official documents.

I found out about my two eldest brothers' deaths by accident though. They were showing some images of the concentration camps on television one day. I was doing some colouring with one of the children in the house. They shifted to photographs of innocent captives and on the second image, I saw the two of them. Gaunt. Their bones sticking out from under their long shirts. No trousers. Their thick hair had been cut to a short buzz. They had smiles on their faces as they stood next to other men, but their eyes were sad. They looked so broken. They were one of the first to go and I think that was a slight blessing. They didn't have to see how bad things got. How low humanity fell.

There have been very good parts and very bad parts but, in the end, I love life. I appreciate it so much more. I picked up my ballet and stuck to it this time. My family made a lot of sacrifices because they thought that I'd be a star, so I didn't want to let their sacrifice for me to be in vain. I was cast in many productions and at the end, a hat would be sent around to collect for those who lost family in the war. I've worked with so many refugees in my spare time. Many of the little boys reminded me of my brothers, so I went back as much as I could so that I could be reminded of them just that little bit more.

My ninety-three years have been very full. I was an awarded ballerina. I had a husband and two children. Every night before I sleep, I ask God for a few more years – I want to make it to an even one hundred. I recite a blessing that my mother gave me on the day I left Poland. It was the last time I heard her say anything to me and I've been reciting it in Hebrew every night since. "Wherever you go, may people always recognise that you have a beautiful heart."

They're words that I have spent most of my life trying to live by.

A Flash Through Me
Birmingham, England

Meredith's Story

Well, where to begin.

I left home when I was twelve years old. I was not a wanted child. My stepmother had no desire to raise me. To her, I was someone else's problem. It was tough. I used to watch my stepmother's children getting soft teddy bears and brand-new dolls. When it came to me, there was never enough money. I had to earn my kept. I used to work as a hired help for our neighbours. I remember one day, I watched my boss's daughter playing with her Barbie doll. She stroked its blonde hair and rocked it like a baby. I grabbed my cleaning brush and copied her. I didn't have any toys to play with, but I had a lot of cleaning equipment, so I tried to do the best I could.

My dad never raised an eye about it. He just wanted to drink his life away. There was a point when his wife had complained so much about me that when a fancy car pulled up asking if there was anyone who could be a servant in his house, my dad didn't even stop to breathe and began negotiating my sale price. I was twelve when I packed my bags to be taken by a stranger to a new country I'd never been to before.

The family in Dubai were very kind to me. They gave me clothes and food. Most of my pay was sent back to my father (a pre-made arrangement), but there was a small amount of money that came my way and I appreciated it. I had some independence there. Some respect. However, things do not remain the same forever. I was growing and becoming an adult. The husband in the house noticed it too. Things quickly began to become uncomfortable. He went out of his way to be around me whilst I went out of my way to not be. He whispered dirty things into my ears and would constantly try to touch me inappropriately. Just the sound of his feet hitting the ground sent shivers down my neck. I tried to ignore the behaviour, but it persisted. I tried to speak frankly with his wife, but she did not believe me and dismissed it. The following week he tried to enter my room every night. I had barricaded the door before I had gone to bed for fear, he would try something like this. I spoke to his wife again. I told her about how he tried to come into my room. About how uncomfortable he made me feel. She wrote me a check and gave me a choice. I could either have a plane ticket to go back home or to London that evening. I couldn't go back home, so I had no option but to go to London.

This was going to be my new start. I kept saying to myself on the plane.

Acton was where I ended up in London. I wasn't really fussed about where I lived, just about the opportunities I could get. I found work very quickly and enrolled into Night College. I had never had an education – I couldn't read or write, and my English wasn't the best. I wanted to learn. Whilst I was there, I met this guy. I played hard to get at the beginning, but he wore me down quickly. He wined and dined me – showing more care towards me than anyone else had ever done in my entire life. After being together for a year, I found out I was pregnant. We'd discussed getting married at some point, so I wasn't worried about telling him. I knew he saw me somewhere in his future but when I told him about the baby, he switched. He was still there but he didn't act the same. He wasn't the warm and happy guy I had met. It was a week before I had my daughter that the world seemed to come tumbling down. I found out that this amazing person who I thought would be 'the love of my life' was already married with a wife and two kids. He had never planned on giving them up. To make matters worse, he wanted out with my child. He had made arrangements weeks ago for her to be sold to his cousin. When my baby was born, I watched her like a hawk. I slept with her in a room that was locked, and I took her everywhere with me. As soon as I was fit enough to move properly, I grabbed my daughter and I got on the first coach out of London that night. No idea where we were going but sure it was better than what we were leaving.

The coach ride was long, but we ended up pulling into Birmingham around one o'clock in the morning. I got out with my daughter in my arms and got into the first taxi I could get, just glad we were finally at a destination. The first thing the taxi driver asked me was 'where to?' and I froze. I hadn't really thought anything through and now I had nowhere to go. No idea where to even get help. I explained my situation to the taxi driver, and he offered to help me. The taxi driver told me that he had a daughter just a little bit older than mine and that he could house me for the night. I had no idea who he was, but I had no choice but to trust him blindly.

That was the best decision I had made for myself since moving to England.

My daughter and I lived with this family for a few weeks. They had five children – four boys and one daughter who was nine months older than my baby. The wife was so kind and caring. It was great to be amongst people that also spoke my mother tongue. Who were understanding of my predicament and wanted to help for no benefit but mine. With them, I felt safe. After a month, they moved me into one of their smaller properties that was close to them in case I had a problem and helped me find work. I remained close friends with both of them as I began to figure out life for myself.

When my daughter was three years old, they sat me down and explained that even though we were in England, I still needed to have additional support. They knew someone who had a wife and child back in Pakistan but was looking to settle down with someone here. I understood where they were coming from and was willing to give it a go. It was a big mistake. The relationship didn't even last three days. The man had perfectly hidden his second mask from everyone. To show that he was kind and caring. He was attentive and a perfect father for my daughter but behind closed doors, he changed. He was violent and continuously suspicious of me. He would question everything I did. Everyone I spoke to. When he didn't get the answers he wanted he would hurt me. I was scared out of my brain that he would hurt my daughter because he had no limit. When he was angry, he didn't leave anything alone. I grabbed our things and moved back in with my friends before I could move out again.

A few years later, I met someone else. He courted me for a long time and was always caring of my daughter. He treated her like his own. We got married and moved to the other side of Birmingham. After marriage, he began to get violent towards me. There were a few times I ended up in hospital but at the time I didn't mind. He was good to my daughter, and we had three boys by then. He was the best father so if I had to make the sacrifice for my kids I would. I didn't have many other options.

When my youngest son was born, we had a christening for him. I had been so busy that day between looking after a crying baby and sorting out the guests, that I hadn't had the chance to attend to my other children. My eldest son hadn't eaten properly the whole day of the christening. I only found that out later because I assumed my husband or his cousin, who we had called over to help with the children after I had complications, was minding them but unfortunately, I learnt too late that this wasn't the case. The next morning, my husband had given him a sip of his drink when he woke up and complained he was thirsty. By the afternoon, he was feeling lethargic and weak. By the evening, we had been waiting for four hours in A and E to find out what had happened to him, only to be told that he had passed away from alcohol poisoning. My life began to crumble away from me. My husband blamed me for his death. He said I should have paid more attention and eventually, he ran off with his cousin (with who he had been having an affair with anyway). I began to try and drink my woes away. Half a glass turned into a whole. A whole glass turned into a whole bottle. A whole bottle turned into a whole box.

My life began to spiral out of control and for years my life was blurred.

All three of my children were being watched by social services because I was turning into an alcoholic and an unfit mother who risked losing all her children. I became depressed out of guilt for my lost child but being threatened with the thought that I might lose the children that I did have permanently, pulled me out. I knew I needed to get real help. I tried to go back to my friends that I had met when I first came to Birmingham. They helped me the first time I'd been struggling that I thought they'd be able to do it again, but I learned too late that they had both passed away. I had no one who could help me but myself.

That's what I did. I helped myself.

I sobered up. I was still illiterate, but I worked four jobs so that I could provide for my kids. I had a 6 am job as a cleaner in a school. At noon I was a lunch lady. After school, I was a cleaner and, in the evening, I was a career for an elderly lady. My daughter dropped out of school at sixteen because I couldn't afford for her not to. I felt bad but when I look at her now, I see how far she has come. My husband came back a few years later after I had struggled so much. He wanted me back, but I now had the strength to say no. I didn't need anyone but myself to support my children and me.

Life was hard for a lot of years. I was trampled on, and I dropped to my lowest several times. The hard years taught me so much though. I grew as a person, and I became the mother I wanted to be. The mother my children deserved.

Our Lives Through a Camera
Islamabad, Pakistan

Fouzia's Story

It seems that violence and pain are the only lens through which ordinary people in Pakistan are viewed in the media. Even if it's a story about a Pakistani rock band, it will be set in the context of a violent society or a dangerous brainwashing of the people.

There's nothing false about that perspective. Pakistan has a problem with violence. Violence is used to silence journalists, judges, moderate religious scholars, and ordinary people. It often feels like it may be getting worse. Every time I see somebody on television speaking out in anger against extremism or corruption – I'll say a prayer for them. Every time one of those people is murdered, those of us who aspire to be like them grow a little more afraid. Women are constantly being portrayed negatively. It seems that any woman or girl that leaves her home in Pakistan, is either abducted, raped, or murdered. Women are only ever harassed, or they will run off with any boy they meet. It's not that the reports of violence or these stories about women are false.

However, they are only a small part of the truth and in the same proportion as any first world country.

There's so much other life being lived here. Most people and places are not like this. Pakistan has some of the most beautiful sights. A world-class army. Some of the brightest people on the planet. The world doesn't see the side of Pakistan that ordinary people see. They don't see that Pakistani people are like a family. In times of crisis, they all come together to help. Just recently, with the case of a raped and murdered seven-year-old child, the people of Pakistan refused to let police corruption ruin the case and prevent the course of justice. People who didn't even know this family petitioned to help. Women have been at the forefront of change, creating awareness of child assault, domestic violence, women's working rights and the importance of education for young women. Girls in Pakistan are not as tightly conserved as many people believe them to be. Times are changing. Girls and women are being allowed to spread their wings. The people of Pakistan are caring more about the integrity of their country. They're caring about their planet, corruption and quality of life.

Nonetheless, there's only so much space in international newspapers. There's so much news in the world so only the most jarring stories make the cut but one day, people will see. Pakistan is very different to the stories that make the cut.

A Masked Disguise
Buenos Aires, Argentina

Florentina's Story

We used to live under a very tight leadership. Our country was full of life and joy before the revolution. We wore bright colours and celebrated both life and death to the fullest. Dictatorship changed that. We were no longer allowed to think for ourselves or find joy in things important to us. It became the government thinking for all of us.

My parents disappeared during the last dictatorship. They were political activists, and their thoughts were considered dangerous and resistant to the ideas being forced at the time. My father was taken first in 1977. My mother was taken a year later during the Football World Cup. I was walking hand in hand with her in a public square when we stopped so she could check which direction we wanted to go. She was taking me to a bakery. We were standing there in plain sight when two cars stopped, and they grabbed us both. They let me go but my mother was never seen or heard from again.

I learned all of this later because I was only three at the time.

My grandparents raised me. When I was a child, they would tell me that my parents were working abroad and that they could not get away yet. I used to imagine what they would be doing and all I could think of was them as architects. Building a skyscraper, wearing helmets, and getting closer and closer to the top. It wasn't until the age of ten that I learned what really happened. I never resented my grandparents. They gave me the best childhood ever and without them, I would have never gone to university, I'd have never graduated, and I'd have never become an architect on my own.

My parents were only ever ideas to me. They were two-dimensional. I didn't remember anything from before the age of four. My only memories were of my grandparents, so it didn't really affect me when I heard they had been killed. My first thought was just...okay.

When I turned seventeen, I visited the town where they first met. It was long after the revolution and the air was buzzing with life and dance. I wanted to get to know them. I wanted to know a part of my history. I found their old friends and spent hours with them. They told me stories about my parents over food and drink. I learned that my mum actually pursued my father. I learned that she was an excellent chef and made the best coffee cake. I learned that my father loved the Beatles and also loved to dance salsa. One of my father's friends gave me a costume that my father would wear when he danced – it was red and black and made of the softest silk.

Suddenly my parents weren't ideas anymore. They were people. For the first time, I cried for them and haven't forgotten them in anything I do. Especially not now, when I'm designing my first-ever skyscraper.

Being a Girl
Paris, France

Clementine's Story

I grew up in a rural town. I was the only girl in the family. Being a girl back then represented a lot of 'no's'. I wanted to study English; the answer was 'no'. I wanted to play the guitar; the answer was 'no'. I wanted to date a boy, but the answer was 'no'. There was a real barrier separating me from life. People had ideas of what girls should be doing or what women should be achieving. Our own opinions did not matter. The only thing my family wanted for me was to graduate high school, get married, become a teacher, and spend every Sunday with them. I didn't want that life, but I found it difficult to stand up to my mama and papa. My family may have been restrictive, but they smothered me with love and happiness. So, I stayed.

After high school, my life became like clockwork. I got married and I got pregnant at twenty-five. I was doing everything I was meant to, but no one was prepared for what would happen when plan A did not work out. My child died during birth. My husband left me because of it.

I felt like I was drowning – completely immersed in the water with no way to get back up.

I don't even remember the passing of time. I lost an entire year of my life because I didn't know what to do now. Was I still allowed to come to family dinner on a Sunday? Was I supposed to try and do everything again from the beginning? Could I do what I wanted to, now?

Eventually, I reached a moment where I knew that now was my only chance to make a major change. I didn't want to live the same routine I was living now. I certainly didn't want to repeat my first experience. People thought I was hysterical or needed to seek help, but I felt a freedom I hadn't before. I was no longer tied to someone or something.

I finally left that town and found Paris. Nothing was ever a no for me here because I refused to let it be.

Moving
Moscow, Russia

Olivia's Story

I peeked when I was in primary school. That was when I last felt like I was adequate. I was top of the class. I was doing extra work. I was taking part in extra curriculum activities, and I actually enjoyed everything I did.

Since then, I've always been afraid I'll live a useless life, and nobody will remember me. Everyone became better than me when I reached high school. They connected to things quickly and found their niche. Most people knew what they wanted to be. I had an endless list of possibilities that I could do but I didn't feel a strong interest in anything. I still don't. If I do, it's just a momentary thing and then something clicks, and I drop it. I tried acting. I tried swimming. I tried chemistry but I got bored with all of it.

I'm continuously worried that if I don't choose something soon then I'll leave nothing behind or worse – I'll get left behind.

We only have a certain amount of energy in life. If you don't put it somewhere then it's wasted and then all I'll have is regret and self-loathing. When I have a goal and I'm moving towards it and I reach it, then I feel a little relief. That's what life is to me. A series of goals that you move toward. Right now though, I'm feeling lost. Everyone else is making moves and achieving big things. I know I shouldn't compare but I constantly feel like I'm falling behind. I feel like I'm stopping myself, but I'm trying to change. I'm trying to find a series of things that make me happy.

I don't think it's possible to just become happy now though. I don't think life's that easy. I do think though, that if I keep moving with small steps, I'll achieve something. It might not be significant, but it can be something I'm proud of. If I keep moving, I can forget that I'm sometimes really sad.

Keeping My Sanity
Havana, Cuba

Camila's Story

There's no appropriateness in this country when it comes to childbirth. Our society expects you to have children from the moment you are sixteen – that's when they really start to find you a husband. People start watching your stomach immediately after marriage like you're an animal in a zoo. Soon the questions begin from family, friends, and eventually complete strangers. It's an expectation.

Thankfully, I have a very supportive husband because we went through seven miscarriages and two stillbirths. The pressure from both our families was unbearable and worse because most of the blame landed on me. I was made to drink potions, bathe in holy water, and avoid all women who were unwedded or had miscarriages. It doesn't matter how much education you have. You get to the point where you'll try anything.

You don't feel like a woman anymore.

That's the biggest problem in our society. People make the comments and make you do crazy things, but they don't think of how it affects you mentally. Seeing other women have five children easily whilst you can't even have one. Seeing a girl who just got married conceiving in a matter of weeks whilst you've been trying for years. The worst one is when you have a baby, but it is born with a disability. You feel so hopeless because there is nothing you can do but people still find fault in you.

People don't pray for healthy children in our country. They just pray for children.

After years of trying and an immense amount of pressure, my husband and I finally visited a specialist doctor. His consult was simple. "There's nothing wrong with you Camila. Go on holiday. Enjoy life." We dismissed his opinion because we'd given up. We thought that maybe this was just not for us but nine months later our son Rafaela was born. Today I have three children.

Knowing what women have to face and because of my own difficulties, I try to help women who are going through the same thing. I run a little community called My Sister's Keeper. We offer free therapy and fertility counselling for women who are having trouble. We offer to help women who want to try and have a child but mainly it's a place to cool off. To get a free spa treatment. To feel like a woman. Some women just want to escape the pressure of the outside world. We provide a safe space for women to think about anything but having a baby.

A Woman's Toolkit
Birmingham, England

Zehra's Story

There was this one day that I had had enough.

I had been asking my husband to get some supplies and food from the shops for a few days but, for some reason or another, he just hadn't achieved this. I understood he was busy with work, but I worked too and had to run a house at the same time. He went to take a nap and said he would take me to the market afterwards, but the clock was already pushing five o'clock and I had to have dinner ready by seven for my five very hungry children.

Putting on my winter coat and tying the scarf around my neck, I grabbed two of my sons to come with me. I had lots of work to get on with and having to wait around for my husband was not an option – especially when I had been waiting for him for a few days. I had watched my husband on many occasions drive his Audi, an automatic, silver car. He made it seem effortless. He moves it to P when he wanted to park and D when he wanted to drive. A couple of times he had told me about the peddles on the floor. I didn't think it would be too hard.

Accelerate. Break. Accelerate. Break.

I kept repeating it to myself as I got the kids into the back of the car, and I sat in the driver's seat. I put the key in and started the engine. After a small prayer, I began my journey. I did all the motions that my husband did whilst he was driving. After the grocery shop and supermarket shop, we got to the meat shop. I parked the car on the road outside. When I got out, I felt a sense of pride. I did a great job for someone who hadn't really driven before and didn't hold a driving licence.

The problem was when we had to go home.

When I walked out of the shop, I could see the car had been tightly blocked in. One car in front and one car behind with a few centimetres between them. I didn't want to damage the car because I knew we couldn't afford a new one or pay to repair either of the car beside ours. My boys helped me put the shopping in the boot and after putting them into the back seat of the car, I stood there trying to work out how I would pull the car out. I was confident enough to drive it on the road, but not confident enough to pull it out of the parking spot. Even my husband sometimes struggled with tight spots, and he'd been driving for a good few years.

Whilst I was standing there stressed and looking at my watch every few minutes, a gentleman from across the road got out of his car and came over to speak with me. He asked me what was wrong and if there was any way he could help. I thought about it for a moment. I knew I wouldn't be able to get the car out by myself unless one of the other cars moved and if this man damaged either of the cars whilst getting mine out for me, then it would be his fault and not mine.

I replied, "I urgently need to get home before my husband finds out that I've gone out, but the car is parked too tightly for me to move it. My boys in the back of the car are really tired too. I don't know what to do."

He told me it was no problem, and he could assist me. He got into the driver's seat and after a lot of back and forth with the steering wheel, he had successfully managed to pull the car out and left it in the middle of the road for me to get into.

Holding my car door open for me and gesturing me to get in, he seemed really pleased with himself for being able to help me out. I was relieved that I could now go home and do the rest of the jobs I needed to do without having to wait for someone to help me. As I got in the car, the gentleman closed the door for me. I rolled down my window as I admired how smart he looked in his uniform and I said to him, "Thank you, officer, you've been really helpful to me today."

The police officer waved at me through my rear-view mirror as I began my smooth car ride back home, thanking my lucky stars he didn't ask for my driving licence.

Green-Eyed Beauty
London, England

Khadeeja's Story

It was hard transitioning from showing my hair every day to wearing a headscarf. A lot of people would debate whether it was appropriate for someone of my age (nine years old) to even be wearing one, but this was my religious requirement. Although there were also many other obligations, this one was one that I looked forward to the least. However, when I actually thought about it, the scarf was never the problem. It was the people. It was myself.

Why was I doing it though?

Alongside the mixed feelings of nervousness and excitement that this stage of my life brings in general, I was growing older, taller, wiser, hairier, and more independent. Sociologists define this stage of life as 'early adolescence', while Islam defines it as *Baligh*. This age might be different depending on which school of thought you follow but the one most agree with for girls is the age of nine. That time had come for me. Where everything my mother, who I was solely dependent upon with every aspect of survival from drinking milk to being bathed, is now experiencing change and I now had to be allowed to experience changes for myself. Becoming *Baligh* is the age that signifies the mental, physical, and spiritual growth whereby a child becomes a Muslim adult. Every child becomes an adult but the tricky part for me was that I now had religious obligations which were compulsory. Things like praying regularly, fasting, paying Khums (a percentage of my savings to charity) and practising Hijab – both physically and emotionally. There's a big misconception that the hijab is just a scarf on my head. My hijab included modesty in my clothing and my behaviour. I am free to have fun and enjoy myself, but I now also needed to be socially aware of what I was saying and how I was behaving. Religiously, I was also my own person. Being Baligh, meant that my opinions and views had to be my own and not my parents. Of course, I could ask for their opinions but ultimately, I needed to have looked up the matter myself and decided. Life was now about balancing my religious beliefs with my social beliefs. Finding a mix between my belief and myself.

For most of my life, the first thing people have ever said to me was 'wow aren't you a pretty girl'. Whether it be because of my large, green sparkling eyes or just my looks as a whole, I was really ever known for being pretty. It was what people remembered. It was all I thought I had. I remember, there was a time when I was a lot younger, I would go into a shop with my family, smile and walk out with a free carton of juice or a packet of sweets. What was I going to be with a scarf on?

I had gone to my Mosque classes every Saturday for two years prior to my transition into year 4. I wore a headscarf there. I found it annoying. It fell off my head. My hair kept coming out. I kept thinking, *does my head look big in this?* The mosque was a steppingstone to wearing the scarf full time but I didn't want to move any further than Saturday morning.

When school started in September, I knew I had to wear one full time – there was no point in fighting it. I had gotten used to putting it on my head and fixing my scarf – practising over the summer holidays. I even got used to how weird it looked on me, but I was still scared. I was anxious because I thought no one would like me now or that everyone would treat me differently. You hear about the stories in the news about women being shouted at or girls being sent home from school because of their scarves. I was nervous this was going to be me.

Everyone else my age or even a little bit older didn't wear a scarf either, so all I saw in my head was my mum and my sister and a lot of older people wearing a scarf but no one that I could relate to. No accomplice of my own.

It was a relief when I came home from school that first day. No one cared about my scarf. My friends still just wanted me. Georgia and Izzie still hugged me tightly and even wanted to try one on for themselves. They wanted my humour, my enthusiasm, my laughter. I realised that I was worried about what other people would think of me – if they'd still like me for my looks, when the real problem was me. I felt that all I had was my looks. I didn't see my personality and when I did, I didn't feel like it was enough to carry me through. My scarf has taken away my vanity of it. There's been a real liberation to me wearing a scarf. Yes, it's still annoying having to run and grab it when some male walks in or I have to go out anywhere, but I'm not as conscious of the way I look. I'm more aware of how to act. I'm kinder. I'm bubblier in my personality. I've not been limited at all. In fact, I hope one day I can be a doctor (well, that's the plan for now anyway).

I still have big green eyes and I'm still a pretty girl. I'm still myself at my core but now I have a personality that people recognise, and a brain people give me far more credit for.

Acknowledgements

Trying to write this acknowledgment made me question how I had managed to write a book. Writing a book is hard, but the acknowledgments seem to be even harder. Not because I don't know where to start but because I'm so very grateful to everyone who made this possible that I don't think I have enough words to express how thankful I truly am.

First and foremost, I would like to thank my grandmother, Sultana Hasnain. I never got to know my grandmother, but without her, this book would not have had a beginning or an end. I'm eternally grateful to her (and my grandfather, Mohammad Raza Hasnain). Thank you for the memories told like tales to your children – my mama held onto them and passed them down to me like fables which I hope will continue to live. Thank you for taking the big (brave) step of moving to England and providing for your kids (and the generations that came from them). Thank you for your sacrifices. Thank you also to my paternal grandfather, Syed Nusrat Ali Shah Bukhari, who has never stopped little ol' me from running around the kitchen, turning on all the taps, making a racket around the house, and 'collecting' things in my numerous shopping bags. Chacha Peera, thank you for loving this pari for who and what she was. Loud. Imperfect. Full of beans. But happy, content and loved. Although I am sad that none of you will ever get to read my stories, you are my stories, and I hope I make you proud through them.

To my mama, Julie. Thank you isn't enough. She has formed every inch of my tapestry and worn many hats – from a confidant to a best friend, to an editor, and a mother. Life is hard and tiring, but you've always seen the positive in it. Thank you for encouraging me to see the fresh blooms of spring during my dreary winters, and for encouraging me to write my own stories, using my wild imagination. Mama, you've tolerated several temper tantrums, proofreads, and stood by me during every struggle and success. I know I'm not easy to deal with, but thank you for listening to me, feeding me, plying me with coffee and tea, and just loving me in general. I used to think I had nothing on paper, just things in my mind, but you've always encouraged me to believe in myself and the dreams I've been dreaming of. It's a magical bond we share. Love you always.

To my siblings Rohail, Bilal and Khadeeja. I've mentioned you in my acknowledgments because Mama said I really should. So here it is. The three of you annoy me and get on my nerves, but you're also so supportive of me, and my writing and are sources of some of my best laughs and greatest memories. You've given me advice on how to take my writing forward (looking at you bhaijaan) and have been some of my biggest champions (thanks Bilal for spreading my writing amongst your friends at uni). Along with Baba, you've provided me with much-needed distractions when things have gotten tough (thanks Khadeeja for introducing me to the world of Korean dramas), and you've always been there for me when I've needed you. I will always be appreciative to have you. Thank you (and my dear siblings, please don't expect any royalties from me).

Thank you to the woman I have always seen as my grandmother, Brenda Sibtain. Your voice message after you read this book gave me the jolt of adrenaline to not give up when I was so close to doing so. Your voice and presence spark such gratitude and love in me. Thank you for everything – for all the hot chocolates you made me when I was little and for accepting I would be making a mess around your house, for reading my first ever book when I was fourteen and telling me I had a chance at creating something wonderful, and for still spurring me on in every facet of my life. You're an incredible woman, and I'm so lucky to have you (and Azhar Nana) in my life.

Thank you also to my family. My mamus Bobby, Hashim and Aftab who have all been constants throughout my life. My Nomi mami. My phuphos Zara, Neeli, Mano, Naheed and Ruby. My Sunny chachu who has never been further than a phone call away. My cousins (particularly Hiba who is always willing to read the early drafts of my work). To my Suzanne auntie, Nilam auntie and all my other aunts and uncles who have been there for me over the past few years, thank you. It's always nice to have people to just talk to and ask how you are. Thank you to my kitties, Shadow, Astro and Luna. I love you and your warm cuddles during long writing spells and TV viewing.

To Lindsay, my plant-loving, coffee-drinking, baking bestie. Thank you for always listening, for helping me to find a reason to buy more plants, for providing a small army of baked goods tasters, and for injecting small rays of sunshine into my day (and sweet tooth). My friends Amy, Jennifer, Jess, Laura, Danuta, Shemin and Katherine. You've always encouraged me to do what makes me happy, provided me with endless laughs and distractions in our chats, and always been ears that listen. Thank you.

Thank you to all the people at my mama's workplace. For eating my endless batches of stressed goods when my writing has hit a brick wall, and for cheering me on (even when you knew nothing about me besides my name and the endless anecdotes from my mama. I'd particularly like to thank Jodie and Kizzy, who read multiple copies of my book and never failed to encourage me to release it to the world. I'm extremely grateful for your support and friendship.

It would be remiss of me to not also mention my library teacher, Mrs Jane O'Sullivan. Without her, I would never have decided to write even a sentence of a book, let alone a whole novel. Thank you for seeing a kid, hungry to find her own little space, hungry to prove she was worth more than she thought and hungry to succeed. She never stopped me; only playfully teased and encouraged me.

To everyone at Austin Macauley Publishers, who enabled me to hold a physical copy of my year-long hard work, thank you so much. I owe everyone cupcakes for all the work and effort you have put into helping my book come to life and I couldn't be more grateful. Thank you.

Writing can sometimes feel like a solitary ride – just my own little world of characters, who speak only the language I have thought out for them – but with so many of you there, it's nice to know that my words and stories are more than just lonely ink on a page.